Clockbreakers

Asterion's Curse

Clockbreakers
Asterion's Curse

KATE RISTAU

Hope Well Books
Oregon

This book is a work of fiction. Names, characters, locations and events are either a product of the author's imagination or are used fictitiously. Any resemblance to any actual event, locale or person, living or dead, is purely coincidental.

First Hope Well Books edition published
November 2017

All production design is a trademark of Hope Well Books, an Imprint of Parenthetical Publishing, and is used under license.

Cover design by Lee Moyer
Manufactured in the United States of America
ISBN 978-0-9908507-5-5

For Mom

For showing me all the worlds
within the words

Also by Kate Ristau

Shadow Girl

Commas: An Irreverent Primer

Find out more at KateRistau.com

CHAPTER ONE

There are a few things you need to know about me. First, my name is Charles Kleis the 15th. And I'm a girl. My dad said that the first child in the family had to be named Charles – always had been, always will be – no matter what. So here I am: Charles Kleis the *Girl.*

Mom calls me Char. Dad seriously hates that. Everyone else calls me Charlie.

Maria looked my name up online. She says it means "free man," and it's not just a boy's name. I reminded her it says "man," but she ignored me. She thinks I'm breaking down barriers, taking down names, and one day, I'm going to rule the world.

Trent explained that the only thing I'm going to rule is the stupid name contest. But he was just mad because I clobbered him on the math speed test. Nobody ever beats me on the speed tests. Not even the fractions. I leave them in the dust.

But I'm moving too fast. Mr. Julian always says to tell them what they need to know first. Don't start right in the middle. So, like I said, my name is Charlie. I'm eleven years old with bright blonde hair and a big gap between my front teeth. It helps me whistle really loud.

I guess I should also tell you I'm in a wheelchair. I don't really care anymore, but other people seem to, so you'll probably want to know too. My legs don't work – not since second grade. But my wheelchair is wicked fast, all black wheels and shiny spokes, and I can outrun any kid in my class (except Maria – she's an all-star!). So, the wheelchair's not that big of a deal. Seriously, it doesn't even get me out of gym class.

Nothing gets you out of Mr. Anderson's class. He has me doing push-ups against the wall, over and over again, even though I tell him it's not doing anything.

"Twenty more push-ups!" he yells.

"Yes sir!" I yell right back. That's fine with me. It's not like I'm missing anything with the leg stretches either.

Anyways, I have a dog named Cordelia and two yellow finches. I live at 232 Glastonbury Lane in Generation, Illinois. My teacher is Mr. Julian, and my favorite color is blue.

Oh, and I met a minotaur.

I know. You want to know about the minotaur. I mean, body of a man, head of a bull? Who wouldn't want to hear about that? And I'll get to it. I will. But there's a lot more you need to know about first.

It all started the day I turned eleven years old. You see, my grandfather, Charlie Kleis the 13th, decided he was going to throw me a party. And not a regular party, either. He was planning one of those all-out torture-fests complete with singing, Aunt Melda's stories, and, of course, the slide-show. One hundred pictures of me eating, laughing, and trying to hide from Grandfather's camera. One hundred pictures of me I would rather everyone didn't see.

I could just imagine what Trent would say as Grandfather displayed pictures of me in my diapers. Probably something like "Nice shorts, Kleis." Then he would smile really big and everyone would laugh. Stupid Trent.

Whatever. It was going to be a long night, with no quick escape. Turning eleven is a real big deal in my family. When my cousin Rachel turned eleven, Grandfather bought her a pony. Seriously, a pony. She squealed.

"What's she gonna do with a pony?" I asked.

"Probably talk it to death," Maria replied.

"Yeah! She'll be all like, 'Hey pony! I love your hair. Where'd you get it done?'"

"And then she'll ask the pony about her shoes and what she thinks about blue eye shadow."

"Is it too much color for someone with brown eyes?"

Maria laughed. "We should go call the animal abuse hotline right now."

"Wait," I said. "Let's at least pet the thing first."

I have to give it to Grandfather – that pony *was* pretty cool.

You know, he's always giving presents like that, and he loves throwing parties: insufferable, never-ending parties.

Hey, don't get me wrong, his parties are usually awesome. I just hate it when all that attention is focused on *me*.

I've had enough of that these last few years. Counseling, physical therapy, careful conversations. And a party – well that was just bound to turn into an "Are-you-doing-okay?" festival.

That was everyone's favorite question for me. They'd see me and their brow would furrow and they'd look real serious and they'd say: "Oh, Charlie. Are you doing okay?"

I'm fine. And I am so sick of being asked.

Still, I was anxious to see what Grandfather was planning. You see, Grandfather lives on the rich side of town. The *really* rich side of town. Where there are gates around all the houses and each garage has more than four cars in it.

We live on the other side of town. In a small house. With one car. Dad works as a production engineer, and Mom is an artist. Not the kind you're thinking of, though. She does *performance* art. That means instead of painting the Mona Lisa, she might reenact it – for four hours – dressed up as a giant bee.

Maria says Mom does charades professionally. I say I've never seen anyone actually pay her.

A couple of months ago, when we were eating take-out from the Golden Garden Restaurant, I asked Dad why we can't just be rich like Grandfather.

"We *are* rich," he said. "In our own way." He adjusted his glasses and smiled at my Mom. She smiled back at him, eyes glistening.

"I don't want to be *that* kind of rich," I said, rolling my eyes. "I want to be rich like Grandfather. With cooks, and maids, and my own gatekeeper."

Dad slowly placed his fork down next to his box of noodles. "Maybe you will be some day. But until then, you should be happier with what you have."

I paused for a moment, thinking about what he said. "I *am* happy," I said, sticking my fork into my fried rice. "But how do you know I couldn't be happier?"

Dad picked his fork back up and stirred his noodles. He had a distant look in his eyes. He opened his mouth, but then quickly closed it. He didn't eat anything, but he didn't say anything either.

"You know, Charlie," Mom finally said, "not everyone wants to be rich like Grandfather."

"That's stupid. *Everyone* wants to be rich like Grandfather."

She sent me to my room.

But they were both missing the point anyway. You see, Grandfather's not just rich. He's *really* rich. Like Bill Gates rich. And his house is like nothing you've ever seen. There are tall spires and large windows and at least seven different wings.

But his house is real weird, too. Some of the doorways are super big, and others look like the only thing that could fit would be a leprechaun. And then there's the parlor. You have to slide open glass doors to get into it, and it has this disgusting orange shag carpeting and dead deer hanging on the walls. But on the other side of the room, there's this giant, sparkling green marble archway that leads to the

Rose Wing and the cherub fountain. All the rooms and all those wings just don't fit together right. It's like someone kept adding them on over the centuries.

As we drove over to Grandfather's house on the afternoon of my birthday, I grilled Mom about why his house looked like that.

"Like what, Char?" Mom asked.

"Charlie," Dad said.

"Like it's not all one house," I said. "Like it's so many different houses."

"It's old," Dad said. "Ancient, in fact. Your grandfather's grandfather had it shipped over from the old country. It took over the top of a whole steamer. That must have been quite an enterprise! They sailed over the Atlantic and up through the Gulf of St. Lawrence and through the Great Lakes and down the Rock River and they didn't stop until the rivers did. And that's how the house got to Generation."

"It's old," I said.

"It is." Dad put the car in park and shut off the engine. "That house seems to have a life of its own. Why, I remember—"

Dad paused and stared at the road ahead, his words gone.

He did that a lot. He would be right in the middle of something – usually something real interesting – and he would wander off. Disappear into his own head. I knew it was no use trying to bring him back. He'd never get through the rest of the story anyway.

"Who's going to be at the party?" I asked Mom instead.

"Your grandfather invited the whole family and all your friends."

"*Which* friends?" I asked, tugging on the edge of my new purple glove, already dreading her answer.

"Maria," Mom said.

I sighed with relief, but in the silence afterward, I knew there was more. "And?"

"And Rowan and Grace."

"And?" I asked again.

"Trent," she said.

I groaned. "Mom! Trent? Why? I thought you said he invited my friends!"

"Trent's your friend," Dad said, a blank look on his face.

"No, he's not!"

"Well, his mother works with your dad," Mom said, unbuckling her seatbelt. "Such a wonderful woman. I've been thinking of performing with her—"

"But it's *my* birthday. I don't see why Mr. Pottypants has to be there."

Dad snapped back to life. "Do NOT call him that, Charles. It's rude."

I knew it was rude. And childish. And immature. But you know what? I didn't care. "Why not? He peed his pants in the second grade. Everyone remembers."

"Then I don't think you need to remind them, young lady," Dad said, catching my eye in the mirror before opening his door.

"Fine. I won't call him Mr. Pottypants," I said. Dad slammed his car door shut, and I crossed my arms, sliding deeper into my wheelchair. "But I'm not going to be nice to him."

Dad pulled my door open and unclipped the tie-down on my wheelchair. "Yes," he insisted, "you are."

His jaw flexed and his eyes narrowed.

I clenched my teeth. "Fine, I am."

But I wasn't. Not really. If Dad knew the real Trent Baran, he'd understand why.

Trent's a jerk. Pure and simple. He whispers bad things about me behind my back. He says my blonde hair is stringy. That my clothes don't fit. That I'm weak. That I'm dirty. Last month, he told our entire homeroom that I tried to kiss Bobby after the football game. He said I pulled Bobby into my lap and wouldn't let him out of my wheelchair until he laid one on me. So gross. Like I would. I can't stand Bobby.

But Trent doesn't care. He's stupid and he's awful.

He wasn't always that way, though. He used to hang out with me and Maria all the time. We'd play cards during recess, go to the movies, and fight to sit next to each other in math class. We were inseparable.

But that was last year – before his parents got divorced.

After his parents got divorced, I tried to talk to him about it.

"You doing okay?" I asked. I didn't mean to ask that question. I *hate* that question. But it was the only thing I could think of.

"I'm fine," he said.

"Really?" I asked.

"Yeah," he said.

Not the most revealing conversation. But I didn't want to press too hard. I wanted to give him his space, right?

After a couple of days, I asked him if he'd seen his dad lately, which I thought was a much better question, and, well, I guess you could say he lost it. He started saying mean stuff to me. Super mean stuff. Stuff that got him sent to the office. Stuff I shouldn't repeat. Stuff I don't want to repeat.

My therapist, Geneva, says I put up too many walls – that I don't deal with my emotions. That I should talk to Trent about what he said and how it made me feel.

I told her, "I'm so sick of talking about it. We are *always* talking."

"That's the point of therapy, Charlie. We talk things through."

"Well, it's not very therapeutic for me."

"Interesting. Let's talk about that."

Talk, talk, talk. I didn't want to talk about what Trent said. I didn't even want to think about it.

And it didn't matter anyway. Right after that, Trent started missing school and getting in trouble. He even got suspended one time for breaking our classroom door. With his fist.

I still kept trying to be friends with him, but honestly, I wasn't sure if I wanted to be. He wasn't the Trent I grew up with.

When he came back to school this year, though, something had changed. He was different. Funny again. Smiling more. But distant. That didn't change anything, though. He still ignored me and Maria. Or he was a total and complete jerkface.

Last week, at school, Maria and I walked past the soccer field, and Bobby yelled at us to go back to computer class.

Trent joined in. "Nobody wants you here!" he yelled. "Go play with your laptop!"

Maria threw her fist in the air. "*Chicos,* I'll show *you* how to play with your laptops!"

I'm not really sure what that meant, but Trent turned back toward the field and suddenly got really into putting on his cleats.

That's the New Trent. He's all into sports now. Soccer, baseball, hockey. He even started doing judo after school.

And I'm cool with that. Honest. It took a while, but I am. I mean, I'm happy he's happy again.

But…I don't get why he can't just be happy with us.

When he does decide to talk to me, it's all sass, smirks, and side comments. With his stupid brown hair that always gets in his stupid blue eyes when he's glaring at you. And his smile. Ugh. You know that if you see his teeth – his perfectly white, beautiful teeth – he's up to something. And it's not going to be good.

Geez, stupid Trent.

My parents don't realize a thing though. He's always super-nice in front of them. And, for some dumb reason, he answered the door for my party.

He locked eyes with my Dad and stuck out his hand. "Oh, Mr. Kleis! It's great to see you." He pumped Dad's hand while Dad nodded his head.

"Good to see you too, Trent," Dad said.

"And good evening, Mrs. Kleis," he said, pulling my

mom into a hug. She laughed, and then I saw it. Just as Trent pulled back, his beautiful white teeth broke into that smile. That awful smile. That dangerous smile. "And you brought your wonderful daughter," he said, and his eyes caught mine. "Happy Birthday, Charlie!"

Happy birthday, indeed.

CHAPTER TWO

My dad nudged me, so I rolled my eyes and mumbled, "Thank you, Trent. Is Maria here yet?"

"Yes. She's at the cheese table." He smiled wryly and held out his hand to me. "I'll show you where."

I shook him off. "Thank you, but no. Maria and I have important matters to discuss."

"Charles—" Dad started.

Trent smiled bigger.

"Fine." I wished I could knock that smile right off his face. "Let's go."

Dad grabbed the handles of my wheelchair and stopped me.

I hate it when he does that. It's so annoying. I mean, can't he get my attention some other way? I spun around to sass him, but when I caught the look on his face, I closed my mouth.

He leaned in and spoke in a low voice, his glasses

pressing into the side of my face. "Please do not head off too far tonight. Your grandfather and I have something to discuss with you. Something important. Stay in this wing."

I nodded quickly and spun around, but he grabbed my handles and turned me back toward him again. Now I was really getting mad.

"Dad—"

"Charlie," he interrupted. "Do me a favor, please?" He had a strange look on his face, like he knew I wasn't going to listen to him.

"What?"

"If…if anyone asks you—" He stopped, wiped his mouth, and started again. "Please, I know it's your birthday party, but please, just…make good choices."

"Dad, give me a break. I'm not a baby—"

"I know, Charlie. Trust me, I know. But, well, just don't talk to any strangers, okay?"

"Really?"

Dad straightened up, pushing his glasses up his nose. "I'm not joking. If anyone comes around—"

"I have your permission to not talk to them. Understood. Awesome. Does that count for family, too? Like Aunt Melda?"

"Be serious, Charlie."

"I am being serious. Give it a rest. It's my party. It's not like anyone—"

"I just want you to be safe."

"Dad. I'm at a birthday party. I'll be fine. Stop treating me like I'm a baby."

"I'm not—"

"Yes. You are. You pull me whichever way you want me to go. You tell me who I should and shouldn't talk to. You never listen to what I have to say. Seriously, Dad. You're always in a mood, and it's always about you. Just leave me alone."

I tried to pull away from him, but he held tight to the handle of my chair. "Charlie—"

"Let me go. You're being such a jerk. Maybe *you're* the one I shouldn't be talking to."

I glared hard at him, expecting him to snap back at me. To freak out. I braced myself for a lecture about character and kindness.

But instead, his face crumpled, and he put his hands through his hair.

Which wasn't right. He should have been angry. Mad. Not sad. Not shaken. Not this. I went back over the words in my head. They felt like squishy balls of day old cheese.

All those stupid words. That is why I never talk. That is why I just want to keep it all inside.

"I'm sorry," I said.

My words felt hollow as he lifted his eyes toward mine; they gleamed behind his dark glasses. He opened his mouth to say something else, then closed it and nodded again.

I'd gone too far.

He patted my head and walked away. I watched him leave, trying to say something else, not knowing what to say. He hadn't even raised his voice. Not once. It wasn't like him at all.

He disappeared into the crowd, but the feeling didn't go

away with him. I rubbed my neck hard, staring off into the crowd, and I caught Mom looking at me. She just shook her head and walked away without a backward glance.

Ugh. Parents. They have the unique ability to make you feel terrible about yourself.

I rubbed my neck harder, staring at Mom as she walked away. There was nothing I could do now. We'd talk about it later. That's probably *all* we would talk about later.

I was already imagining how Mom would make me draw a picture of Dad's feelings using leftover macaroni and cheese. She might even get out the spaghetti sauce. And Dad would insist I reread *The Giving Tree*. He says it has a great moral about friendship and giving and kindness.

I say the boy mutilates the tree, stealing its apples and cutting its branches, and, in the end, he *sits* on it. Doesn't really feel like a story about kindness.

But we would talk about it. And Geneva would talk about it too. We'd all talk about it.

At least they wouldn't ground me.

I sighed and wheeled toward the cheese table. Maria would know what to do.

My chair shook. "Ouch!" Trent yelled.

I looked down and saw his foot behind my wheel. I started to say I'm sorry, but when I glanced up and saw the stupid look on his face, I rolled my eyes instead.

"I love your new gloves," he said. "Seriously. The purple looks really great with your green shirt. And so much better than those stupid batting gloves you usually wear."

I clenched my fist. I liked my new gloves. Mom usually

gave me some stupid present. Like a globe covered in melted chess pieces. Or seven Pepsi cans full of red buttons. The gloves were the first gift that actually made sense. Sure, they were opera gloves, but at least she was trying.

I wouldn't let Trent make fun of my gloves. They were mine. And he was a loser. I laid into him. "Oh, Mr. Kleis! It's *so* great to see you—"

"I'm sorry for interrupting your 'important matters' with your best friend. Does it involve cheese? That's all Maria seems to have on her mind."

I looked over at the cheese table and caught Maria's eye. She looked like she was in heaven. Her slim, athletic figure was bent over the table, and her mouth was stuffed full. To be clear, Maria's lactose intolerant mouth was stuffed full of cheese. Again.

This was not going to be a good night.

"I have to go," I said.

Trent smirked and pointed in Maria's direction. "Tell Fartface over there to lay off the cheese. For the sake of the other guests."

"As you say, Mr. Pottypants."

His face turned bright red, and I made my escape before he could get another word in.

I wheeled over to Maria, grabbed the piece of cheese right out of her hand, and shoved it in my mouth. "You shouldn't be eating this," I mumbled through the cheese.

"Your grandpa shouldn't have a whole table devoted to *queso,* Birthday Girl. I mean, is he *trying* to kill me?" Maria pointed toward her stomach, which she had slipped into a pair of skinny jeans.

They were bright pink.

Only Maria could make those look good. It didn't matter what she ate. She never got fat, even though she pigged out all the time. She was gorgeous. Long, dark curly hair and dark skin. And so tall.

But she'd really be regretting that cheese later.

"I don't care what—" She stopped suddenly and looked me in the eyes. "Are you okay? What happened?"

"Nothing. I'm fine."

She tilted her head and waited, tapping her foot.

"Dad," I said. "Just Dad. Always treating me like a baby." Over her shoulder, I saw Aunt Melda heading toward us. "Let's get out of here. Melda's coming."

Maria stole one last piece of cheese, pushed it in her mouth, and then grabbed the handles of my chair and wheeled me around toward the nearest exit.

We were almost free when I saw a flash of yellow, and then Aunt Melda fell upon me.

"Oh Charlie," she said, diving toward my chair and pulling me into her chest. "Happy Birthday!"

I mumbled into her shirt, and after a long moment, she released me, crouching down beside my chair. "How are you doing?" she asked.

I cringed at the question, but shrugged it off. "Oh, fine. Good. Uh, really good."

"*Fantástico,*" she said. I smirked at her newest Spanish vocab word. "What a wonderful night for a party! Your Grandfather is very *feliz* you're here. Very happy. We all are so happy you are here."

That was weird. She says weird things. Sad things. But in a really happy voice. She's been like that since the wheelchair. A little edgy – but not in a cool way.

Maria threw her arms around Aunt Melda and pulled her up to standing. "Oh, I am too, *Tía* Melda. *Es un cumpleaños importante para ella. Once años. ¿Es imposible, no?*"

Aunt Melda was nodding her head along with Maria, but when Maria stopped, she started sputtering. "So *feliz*. So *feliz* you're both here. I'm so *feliz*. But cake! I have to get the cake ready! No time to waste. Cake to eat! Birthday!" She turned quickly and headed off toward the kitchen, mumbling something about plates and ice cream.

Maria was grinning. "Her Spanish lessons are really going good, huh?"

"*Más o menos*," I said. "Mostly *menos*. Thanks for getting rid of her."

"*No problemo*."

We were almost to the doorway when someone called my name. I turned and was engulfed in a pile of mascara and frills.

"Where are you going?" my cousin Rachel asked.

"You haven't even said hi to us," my other cousin Kimmy said.

"We even brought you a present," my third cousin Brittany added.

"Thanks guys!" I said. "I can't wait to open it."

Brittany's hand was resting on my wheelchair. "It's a book about computers," she said.

"Because we know you like to read," Rachel added.

"And we don't," Kimmy said.

I cut in before they got another word out. "My dad said he needed to talk to me. Have you guys seen him?"

"Not even," Rachel said.

"Is he here?" Brittany asked.

"Probably working again," Kimmy said.

"He's always working," Rachel insisted.

I didn't take the bait. "Any sign of Grandfather?"

"He's in his study," Kimmy said.

"He said he needed to find a book," Rachel noted.

"But I think he's just trying to get away from us," Brittany added.

I nodded, and pointed toward the door. "I'm going to go see if he knows where my dad is."

"Hurry back," Kimmy said.

"We want you to cut your cake—" Rachel announced.

"So we can eat it," Brittany finished.

As we crossed the foyer, Maria shook her head. "After all these years, I'm *still* not sure which is which. They all look the same to me. And they finish each other's sentences, too. And remember Kimmy's slideshow? *Loca*."

"Yeah, and—"

Suddenly the doorbell rang. Since we were right next to the door, I sighed and yelled, "I got it!"

I pulled open the door. Standing in the archway under a twinkle of green lights was a tall man in a dark suit. He had long, jet-black hair that hung beneath a strange, wide black hat. His eyes – at first I thought they were green, but when I looked again they were purple – shone with an unnatural light. I rubbed my own eyes before mumbling, "Good evening. How can I help you?"

He slowly removed his black hat and took a step closer. "Are you Charles Kleis?"

His accent was thick and strange; it took me a moment to realize he said my name. Or did he mean Grandpa? He probably meant Grandpa. I didn't want to ask, but he was staring at me intensely, waiting for my response.

Dad had just told me – no strangers. And this guy fit the very definition of strange. I didn't want to be rude, though, so I finally answered, "We are having a party. Grandfather is busy."

He cocked his head slightly. "I didn't come here to see your Grandfather. I came here to see you. You *are* Charles Kleis the 15th, are you not?"

"Now, how do you know that?" Maria asked. She had slipped closer to me and was puffing her chest out a little bit.

"I make it my business to know these things, Maria. And an eleventh birthday? Why, that's a very special thing indeed."

It was weird how he knew Maria's name too. His level of creepiness was rising by the minute. I felt a chill go through me as his eyes caught mine, and I thought that maybe I should have listened to Dad.

I gestured for Maria to get the door. "I think it's time you were leaving Mr.—"

"Prom," he replied, pulling his hat from his head and making a small bow. His black hair barely moved. "I'm a…friend…of your grandfather's."

"I'll make sure to tell him you stopped by," I said as Maria closed the door.

He stuck out his black boot and stopped it. I wheeled back as he slithered – that's the best word for it – into the room. "I won't stay long. I just have a present for you, Charlie. A small gift. Nothing but a trifle, really."

"I don't want any presents. And I'm not supposed to talk to strangers," I said. "Maria, could you get—"

"I'm terribly sorry," he interrupted, turning back to the door. "There's no need. I'll just be going. I'm sorry if I've frightened you—"

"*I'm* not frightened." Maria widened the door for him to leave. She looked ready to push him out of it.

"But you *should* be going," I added. "This is a private party."

He turned back toward me, the corners of his mouth slipping upward. "For just a moment, you sounded exactly like your father. Did he tell you to say that?"

I could feel the color rise up in my face. "I'm eleven years old. He can't tell me what to do."

"I couldn't agree more," Mr. Prom said.

Maria grabbed my arm and whispered in my ear, "Let him go. He's creeping me out."

Mr. Prom must have heard her. He looked directly at her, but spoke to me. "Of course. Of course, I'll go. But before I do…" He slipped a chain out of his pocket and dangled it in front of me. On the end of the chain was a small, ornate silver key.

For a moment, I thought there were several keys, but when I blinked, only one danced on the end of the chain.

"A key?" Maria asked.

"A key," he replied.

But he was wrong. They both were. It was more than that. It was beautiful. It was silver and intricate and delicate and elegant. And I wanted it. More than anything I'd ever wished for in my life. It was perfect.

I stared at the beautiful key – the way it danced in the green light. The way it seemed to stretch and strain toward me. The way it twinkled. I swear I even heard it call my name. My fingers itched for it, longed to touch that slip of silver.

"Come on," Maria said, nudging me back to earth. I stared down at my empty hand. Without the key, I felt lost inside, empty. "You know what your dad said—"

"Charles?" Mr. Prom shook his head slowly. "That does sound like him. Always ordering people around. Telling them what to do."

I snapped, a wave of anger rushing through me. "This has nothing to do with him. He's not here. And I don't have to listen to him if I don't want to. It's *my* birthday."

I was so sick of Dad always ordering me around. Treating me with kid gloves. Like I was back in that hospital bed. That was three years ago. I was so much older. Stronger. Different.

Mr. Prom looked down on me, his eyes shining. "It *is* your birthday. And the key belongs to you. It is yours."

"Mine," I repeated.

I know. It sounds really lame when I look back on it. But that's just the way it was. I didn't even think about how weird it was that I couldn't take my eyes off that key. Honestly, I could barely think at all.

In the back of my head, I could hear a smarter, better

version of myself whispering that I shouldn't trust this guy, that maybe I was being a little crazy. Somewhere in the back of my mind I knew I shouldn't want the key that much; it was unnatural.

But in the front of my head, I saw it dangling on the chain, waiting for me. Calling to me. It was practically screaming inside my head.

I didn't know what the key opened. I didn't care. I would take it. I would hide it. I'd grab it in my hands and shut the door, and Mr. Prom would leave, and Dad wouldn't have to know. *No one* would have to know. And Maria wouldn't tell anyone. She's cool like that.

Mr. Prom swung the key in front of my eyes, and I swallowed hard, then reached out to take it, to hold it. My gift. My key. Mine.

But as I stretched out my hand, Mr. Prom pulled it just beyond my reach.

That, by the way, is not a very nice thing to do to a kid in a wheelchair. I glared at him. He ignored it, and my eyes fell back on the key again.

"This key, it isn't exactly free—"

Maria interrupted him. "Well, it's not a present then, is it, *hombre*?"

I could feel Maria nudging my shoulder, but I tuned her out. The key was pulsing, aching for me. It whispered my name again and again.

I ignored Maria, listening to the sound of the key calling to me – *Charlie, Charlie* – and watching Mr. Prom waving it back and forth in front of my eyes. "It comes with a small price. Are you willing to pay it?"

That made me hesitate. It was something about the way that he said it. Maybe I should have just listened to Dad. Maybe I shouldn't have opened that door in the first place. Something wasn't right. But I couldn't figure out what. I mean, I couldn't even focus as I watched the key dancing on its silver chain. It flickered and shimmered and seemed to radiate its own light. Each shining pulse beat along with my heart as it whispered my name. *Charlie. Charlie. Charlie.*

So, I gave in. I relented. Seriously, I would have paid anything to have it in my hands. "What's the price?"

"A strand of your hair."

"Okay, *Señor* Creepy." Maria's voice broke the spell. The key stopped whispering my name, stopped glimmering and pulsing on its silver chain. For just a moment, it looked like a regular key again. "That's enough of that. You might have Charlie fooled, or hypnotized, or something *loca* – but not me. *Nada más.* We'll tell Mr. Kleis you stopped by—"

"Maria!" I shouted. "Wait!" She gave me her *Are-You-Loco* look.

And that's just it. I *know* it was crazy. But that didn't matter. I wanted it. Pulsing or not, that key should have been mine. It was like a part of me that I never knew was missing before. I needed it, deep down. I would pay Mr. Prom's price. I would have that key.

I ripped out several pieces of hair and shoved them at Mr. Prom. "Here." I grabbed the key from his hand.

He stared down at my hair in his hand, and his face seemed to stretch and crack and shimmer, but then it settled into a smile. An awful smile. A terrible, horrible, Disney-villain-type-smile.

"I think you made the wrong choice," Maria said.

Mr. Prom's smile disappeared, and he placed his hat back on his head. "You are wrong, Maria. She could not have chosen better. The world is hers."

With that, he turned and walked down the drive. I never saw him get into a car, or leave the grounds, but I didn't care. My life was complete. The key was mine.

CHAPTER THREE

"I think you made the wrong choice," Maria repeated.

"You already said that."

"I know that, *chica.* I just want to make sure you know too."

I grasped the key by its silver chain and held it up to the light. It sparkled, almost *winked* at me. I smiled, feeling just for a moment like the world was perfect, complete, and that everything would actually be fine. I ripped off my purple gloves and opened the clasp. I sighed as it clicked into place around my neck.

"What does it open?" Maria asked.

"Does it matter?" I responded, testing the weight of it in my fingers.

"Whatever. That's weird. And he was weird. And you're being weird. Ugh, I can't believe you gave him your hair." She suddenly looked very pale. "You're *loca,* girl. Just crazy. And talk about creepy. Your grandfather's friends are so weird." She paused for a moment, grasping her stomach tightly. "But I'll give you a break because it's your birthday. And honestly, I don't feel good. So let's just go find your Grandfather already."

"You shouldn't eat that much cheese," I said, pulling my gloves back on.

"You think I don't know that?"

I could tell she was struggling, but that still didn't slow her down. Nothing can slow Maria down. She nearly danced down the hall as she raved about the cheese, the cake, the cookies, and how much she loved Grandfather's parties.

I only half listened to her. How was I even supposed to focus when that glimmering…thing…hung around my neck? I didn't even know what to call it. Key wasn't the right word. That was too simple. Too ordinary. It was more than a key. It was a sense of possibility. Couldn't she see that? Couldn't she feel it? I tucked the key inside my shirt and pressed it to my chest.

"And the cream puffs! Did I tell you about them? *Muchacha*, I've never had anything yummier. I'm sorry, Charlie, but even if he wasn't your Grandfather, I'd come to his parties just for the desserts—"

"Charlie!"

I turned and saw Grandfather running down the hall. His coat was missing a sleeve, and his glasses were cracked. A streak of blood crossed his cheek.

"Where is he?" he yelled, stumbling toward me. "Did you give it to him?"

The key warmed against my chest. Was Grandfather

talking about Mr. Prom? How did he know—

"The key!" he yelled. "The key! Did he give it to you? Did you pay the price?"

"Yes, I—"

He staggered, but stayed on his feet. "Of course. Of course you did."

I tried to say I'm sorry, but he cut me off again. "There's no time. We have to get to the door. We have to stop him!"

He spun around and ran back into the crowd. I yelled after him, "Grandfather! Where are you going? He went outside!" He must not have heard me. He was already pushing his way through the crowd.

I spun my wheels on the tile, and Maria jumped behind me and started pushing me down the hallway.

But we couldn't move fast enough. There were too many people in the way. Everyone was stopping, talking, chatting. I wanted Maria to just run over them all.

"Oh, Charlie! I haven't seen you all night! Happy Birthday!"

"Thanks, Nathan! I don't really—"

"Well! There you are! The birthday girl! I love that shirt, Charlie!"

"Thanks, Lily. Sorry I can't talk, but I—"

"Cake!" Maria yelled. Her voice bounced down the hallway. "Aunt Melda wants us all in the parlor!"

That got everyone moving. They nodded and smiled at us, gesturing toward the parlor and the cake.

Kleises. All you have to do is say the word cake, and we'll come running.

Maria pushed me behind the crowd, and we slipped past

them into the Rose Wing. Once we were free of all the people, Maria burst into speed.

I couldn't see Grandfather, but we had to be gaining on him. The armor and paintings and pig statues were flying by my chair. Suddenly, we were going so fast, my shirt whipped up, and I had to pull it back down. When I looked up, we were standing in front of Grandfather's study.

"That was so fast—" I stopped, staring at the large oak doors. They were shut, and a giant sword was wedged between the handles – like someone was trying to keep someone – or something – trapped inside.

I didn't have time to make sense of it all. I grabbed the sword and yanked on it as hard as I could, but it was the wrong angle from my wheelchair. "Maria! Pull this out!"

I wheeled out of the way, and Maria wedged one foot on the handle and yanked out the sword with all her might.

"Cool!"

I whirled around. "Not now, Trent."

"Are you kidding? Come on – you can't make me leave now. I *know* that's not a replica. Look at that finishing. And the pommel. Is that your grandfather's? His stuff is awesome. Give it to me. Lemme check the balance." He held out his hand, but Maria shook her head and slowly slipped it between her jeans and her belt buckle, like she did it all the time.

Trent sighed and jammed his hands in his pockets. "What's it doing there, anyway?"

"We were just going to—" Then I heard it. A low grumble. Or a growl.

It was coming from the other side of the door.

"Who was that?" Maria asked.

"*What* was that?" Trent asked.

I paused for a moment, my hand on the door. "Only one way to know."

Maria pulled the sword back out, and Trent slid in next to her. I glared at him, then shoved the door open.

"Grandfather!" I cried. Trent pushed past me and ran to kneel beside my grandfather, who was sprawled on the floor by his desk, his glasses crushed by his feet, his toupee askew. I wheeled up next to him as Trent pulled him up to sitting.

"Are you okay?" Trent asked. "Can I get you something?"

What a suck-up. I hit Trent with my wheel and shot him a shut-up look.

"Your dad—" Grandfather mumbled.

"Is he okay? What were you running—"

"They hurt—" His eyes unfocused and refocused again, and he rubbed his hand slowly across his face, smearing the blood across his other cheek. I waited for him to tell me something – anything. What had happened to Dad?

A wave of guilt washed over me, but I pushed it aside. He was fine. He had to be. "What happened?" I asked.

"The automatons took—" He grabbed my arm and stared at me with startling intensity. "Use the key! Go!" he yelled, pointing to the door at the back of his study.

"Is Dad okay? Should I get—"

"There's no time! Take Trent with you. And Maria too. Find Asterion as fast as you can. Tell him who you are. Tell him you have the key—"

I started and glanced down toward the key. It was still tucked inside my shirt. How did he know?

"What are you waiting for?" he yelled. "They have him!"

My grandfather had never raised his voice to me in my entire life. My stomach flipped in response, and I looked up at Maria. "You coming?"

"Yep." The color had come back into her face, and she was still holding the sword in front of her. She was dancing back and forth on the balls of her feet.

"Me too." Trent's smirk had disappeared.

I glared at him again.

He didn't return my glare. He was already on his feet. He suddenly had his backpack in his hands and was slipping it on.

I shook my head at him. "You're not coming—"

"He said I am—"

"Go!" Grandfather yelled. "Before it's too late!"

When I saw the look on Grandfather's face, I forgot all about Trent. I had to help my Dad. I nodded once at Grandfather, and then wheeled quickly around him until I was right in front of the door.

The door looked really old, with pale wood and dark scratches. I'd never opened it before – I'd never even noticed it before. When I leaned in closer, I realized it was almost like a puzzle that had been painstakingly pieced together. Little shards of wood interlocked, forming a strange door that looked older than anything I'd ever seen. It was ancient.

The keyhole, however, it *shined.* I could feel it tugging on me, pulling on my key. I lifted the key out from underneath my shirt and it almost burned my fingers. It was so hot.

I shoved it in the keyhole. It slid right in. I turned it to the right until I felt a gentle click, then a sharp electric feeling poured through me. I could feel the tips of my fingers, the backs of my hands. Something was about to happen. Something I didn't understand.

I looked up at Maria, who was still balancing the sword in her hand. She smiled and nodded down at me, ready for anything. I gripped my wheels hard, and she pushed the door open.

A wave of power rushed over me, and the room filled with light.

CHAPTER FOUR

I can't even tell you if we crossed the threshold. I just remember how Maria, Trent, and I stared in disbelief. We were in a different world.

We were on a small hill above a giant maze that stretched for miles and miles. The sun beat down on our faces, and the walls of the maze sparkled in the sunlight; they were at least fifty feet high, made of rough-hewn, sandy rock. The walls seemed to grow out of the ground, reaching upward toward the hot desert sun.

Just looking at the maze made me tired. I could see trees and fountains throughout the maze, but what I couldn't see was my Dad. Or a way out. I spun around, and it was the same. Just more and more maze all the way to the horizon.

I looked for some sign of Dad, some flicker of movement in the desert heat, but there was nothing. Nothing but sandstone walls for as far as I could see.

Which didn't make sense. We were in Illinois. Illinois is not the desert. Illinois is farmland. Soybeans. Cows and sheep. Illinois doesn't have a giant maze. Unless it's made of corn. And that's only in October. It was June.

I shook my head slowly as my eyes searched the deep desert maze. Dad had just crossed through the door, right? Why couldn't I see him? If he had just come through, where had he gone?

When I turned back around, the door was shimmering, like it was barely even there. I reached out to touch it, and my hand went straight through.

"Um…what just happened?" Maria asked. When no one answered, she turned back around and spread out her arms. "And where are we?"

"And *when* are we?" Trent mumbled.

"When?" I asked, turning my chair around to face him. "What do you mean 'when?'"

"Look around. Does this *look* like the 21st century?"

Maria spun around and rolled her eyes at Trent. "It *looks* like we're stuck with you."

"Wow, dork," Trent said. "Your powers of observation are mind-blowing."

"You think so, dork?" Maria took a step closer to him.

"I think so, dork," he replied, stepping closer to her.

I waved them both off. "You guys are *both* being dorks. We need to find my dad. Which way did he go?"

Maria and Trent both scanned the maze, eyes squinting in the bright sunlight. After a moment, Trent shook his head. "I don't see him."

"Wait," Maria said, "where's the door?"

I wheeled around, but all I saw was more maze. The door wasn't just shimmering anymore – it was completely gone. Disappeared. Into thin air.

"Where did it go?" Maria ran her hands through the air where the door had been. "Where is it?"

I didn't have an answer. "I don't know."

Trent adjusted the straps on his backpack. "Looks like we're going to have to find some other way."

I turned my wheelchair back around and stared down the hill, where a giant archway led into the maze with its unending rows of rocks. It was the same exact thing for miles around. We weren't going to find some other way. That was the only way. And it looked like it was going to take forever.

I sighed and started to wheel down the dirt path. If that's where Dad had gone, I was going too.

"Wait a minute," Maria said. "You want to go in there?"

I turned back and looked at her. "Do we have any other choices? I mean, Trent's right. The door's gone. Dad's gone. We have to find him. And I don't see another magic door appearing."

"Well, we can at least talk about it before you go charging down the hill," Maria said.

Ugh. That tone. I knew that tone. I hated that tone. It was the Maria-thinks-I'm-too-bossy-tone.

"Fine," I said, gritting my teeth. "Talk."

She threw me a sassy look first. I widened my eyes, and she went on: "Listen, *chica*, we don't have any food. Or water. What are we going to do when we get in there? It's not like we're just running around the block. That maze is huge. It's gonna take, like, forever."

"So it's a food thing then?" Trent asked.

Maria snapped. She pushed Trent hard toward me. I jerked forward, holding my arms out to catch him, but he didn't fall backwards. He just stood there and smiled. "So it is a food thing then."

Maria reeled back to punch him, but I stopped her before things got out of control. "Just knock it off. Both of you. Maria – you're right – we don't have any food. Or water. But we don't really have any other choice. There's no food where we're standing right now either. And we have to find my dad."

The last words I had said to him raced through my mind. Those gross words. Those stupid words. And the look in his eyes. "So, can we just start making our way into that stupid labyrinth—"

"Labyrinth?" Maria asked.

"Yeah," I replied. "Labyrinth."

"Like with David Bowie?" Maria asked, turning her back on Trent. "And Ludo? Why didn't you say so?" She smiled and nudged my arm. "I'd go anywhere for the Goblin King. Remember his hair? And that voice! I wish he'd steal my little brother."

I laughed, pushing my hair off my sticky forehead.

Maria could go from raging mad to happy in four seconds. All you had to do was mention one of her favorite movies. Or give her food. "I wish he'd steal your little brother too," I said.

"I know! You know when she tells him, 'You have no power over me?' She's stupid. I would totally let him have power over me."

"Maria," I said, "he's like eighty!"

"Doesn't matter—"

"Please!" Trent said. "If I'm going to be stuck with you two in a labyrinth for who knows how long, can we at least not talk about David Bowie? Just watching that movie was torture enough."

"I didn't invite you to this conversation, *chumaco*," Maria said, flipping her long brown hair in his direction. "So, you don't need to talk about the Goblin King if you don't want to. And *por favor*, I'd prefer it if you didn't talk at all."

"Well," Trent said, "*I'd* prefer it if we made our way toward one of those fountains in there. Besides, it'll be cooler in the labyrinth."

Maria rolled her eyes at him. "It'd be a lot cooler without you in it."

Trent opened his mouth, but I cut in. "Can we just get going, Maria? I'm sick of sitting around in the sun, too."

"Seriously?" she said. "Who's your best friend here?"

"You," I immediately replied. "Definitely you."

Trent caught my eye, and for a moment, I saw the Old Trent in there. The one that wasn't so angry. The one that wanted to hang out and play video games and get pizza. The one who could smile without making you feel like garbage. But then he turned away.

I sighed and turned away too, following Maria down the hill. My wheels spun in the sand unexpectedly, and I gripped them hard. They shifted a couple of feet and slowed to a stop. I pumped with my arms, and my wheel shifted slowly underneath my new glove. I tightened my grip and pushed harder. My chair is definitely not made for off-roading in loose sand.

I put my hand up to shield my eyes as I examined the archway into the labyrinth. The path was mostly worn-down sandstone. The going would be much easier once we crossed into the labyrinth.

Still, I couldn't believe we were going to do it.

I could almost hear Dad's voice in my head, telling me to slow down and take things as they come. That you don't eat an elephant all at once. You take it one bite at a time. I always thought that was a gross saying, but at that moment, as I stared at those sandstone bricks, I wouldn't have minded him saying it.

I pulled up hard on my glove. I had been so mean to him. The things I had said…the way he looked at me…the way Mom had looked at me…I shook my head hard, trying to get it all out. But I couldn't. It was still there, swimming around in my head. I was just so sick of him telling me what to do all the time. He was always treating me like a baby. Everybody was always treating me like I was so fragile.

But staring into that labyrinth with the weight of the key around my neck, I knew they were wrong. I was stronger than they knew, and I couldn't help but smile. The key…it felt good. It felt powerful, like it could make anything possible.

As I gazed into the labyrinth, my smile disappeared again. Could the key bring Dad back? Could it reach across that unending maze, search through the walls, find him, and bring him back home?

I shook my head slowly and reminded myself: not the whole elephant. One bite at a time.

So, with one last, long breath, I pulled myself up straight, grabbed my wheels, and crossed into the labyrinth.

As I passed under the archway, a cool breeze brushed across my face. It smelled like the beach, and the basement, and – was that rosemary? – all at the same time.

The path stretched out before us, stone walls on each side. The walls were so tall that they threw shadows on the ground. The air cooled my skin, and I smiled. Trent was right. It *was* cooler in the shade of the labyrinth. I looked over at Maria. "He's right. It's nicer in here. Let's give him a break."

She burst into song, and I covered my ears. Maria has a horrible voice, like skull-grating, but that didn't stop her. She belted it out like David Bowie.

I started wheeling further down the path. "All right, all right, let's figure this out. What do we know about labyrinths?"

"They're like giant mazes," Maria sang back off-key.

"Duh, Maria," Trent said.

"Shut-up, Trent," I said.

"No way," he said.

I ignored him. "Maria, remember the maze in *Labyrinth*?"

"Charlie!" Trent said. "Come on. No more Bowie!""

"Sorry – just one more thing. It's just – in the movie, she gets like lost and stuff, right?"

"Yeah," Maria said. "That's kind of the thing."

"But most labyrinths aren't like that." I pointed down

the sandy path. "You usually don't get as many choices in a labyrinth. You're usually forced along one path until you get to the end."

"How do you know that?" Trent asked.

"Mom's show. Remember? She took a banana, used it to draw an outline of a labyrinth, and walked around in it for an hour. She called it 'Banana Foster Wallace.'"

Maria groaned at the memory. "I called it 'Boring.'"

"Man, I'm happy I didn't have to sit through that one…" Trent trailed off and looked away again. Things got really quiet. All you could hear was the scrape of my wheels on the packed sand path.

You see, Mom's show was at the end of last school year. When New Trent decided he didn't want to hang out with us anymore.

The scrape of my wheels on the packed sand path was the only sound for miles around. I looked down at my wheels and really focused on turning them. One rotation at a time. Over and over.

Trent finally broke the silence. I thought he was going to say something about how my mom's art is terrible, or I thought he might even make a joke, but he surprised me.

"Your mom would love this labyrinth."

I nodded slowly. "She would – as long as she had a banana."

Trent and Maria laughed really loud – a lot louder than they should have. It wasn't that funny of a joke. But I laughed too. None of us really wanted to think about what Trent had said.

That's the stupid thing. Even when Trent's being nice,

he just – I don't know. He misses the point. There are some things you just shouldn't say.

And I didn't want to give him another chance to say them. "Moving on, besides David Bowie, what do we know about labyrinths?"

Maria stared at me blankly. Trent looked over at me, too. His face was pale, but he said, "You're the smart one. What do you know?"

"Okay, okay." I looked away, really working on my wheels. "Just let me think. There was a Greek Labyrinth. In the stories Mrs. DePauw used to read to us. Remember? Her scratchy old voice and those mind-numbingly boring stories?"

"Yes!" Maria said. "I remember that one! With the bird man!"

"Icarus," I said. "He escaped the labyrinth. But he flew too close to the sun—"

"And was burned alive!" Maria said.

"Not exactly," Trent said. "The wax on his wings melted and he fell into the sea—"

"The Icarian Sea," I added with a glance over at him.

He smiled at me, and I blushed, pushing my wheels harder again, feeling too hot in the desert heat.

Stupid Trent.

"At least someone was paying attention," he said.

"But I don't get it. Why was he in there in the first place?" Maria asked. She was running her hands along the walls. I watched as little chunks of rocks fell off and bounced underneath my wheels. They ground into dust.

I tried to think of what else I remembered about Icarus.

"He was trapped in there with his dad, Daedalus," I said. "The one who made the labyrinth."

Maria knocked off another piece of the rock wall and grabbed it before it fell. She drew her arm back and launched it up ahead of us, then grabbed another chunk. I lost my train of thought as I watched her rock fly down the path and smash into the wall.

"Yeah, but *why* was he in there?" She grabbed another rock and launched it ahead. "And why would Daedalus trap his own son in there, too?"

My mind drew a blank. I remembered something about Ariadne, but that was it. I swallowed my pride and looked up at Trent.

"You got me," he said. "I only know the Icarus stuff. You know, the bird man?" He waved his arms at Maria and she raised a fist. He rolled his eyes and batted it away. "Give it a rest. I don't remember how they got in there in the first place."

"Why are we talking about this anyway?" Maria asked. "It's not like it matters. It was like 400 years ago."

"Try 4000," I said.

"No thanks." Maria knocked off another piece of wall.

"Maria," I said quietly. "Could you please stop destroying it?"

She looked at me out of the corner of her eye. "No thanks," she said again.

"Come on," I said. "I mean, somebody built all this. We shouldn't just wreck it."

"Charlie," Maria said. "Seriously. We are *trapped* in here. We are looking for your dad. Do you think I really care who made this *laberinto*?"

And that's when it hit me. He was gone. Really gone. Maybe hurt – maybe bleeding like Grandfather – or kidnapped – kidnapped by some crazy guy who gave me a key. A key that brought us here. Through a doorway in my grandfather's house and into another world.

And Dad was nowhere in sight.

But, for a moment, all the strangeness and fear had slipped away. For a moment, I was just talking with my friends. I was remembering those old stories – who was in them and what they had done. The memory of my dad had slipped away, and I had almost forgotten why we were in the labyrinth in the first place. Whom we were looking for. I had almost forgotten Dad was gone.

Almost.

"Charlie's got a point," Trent said, bringing me back to reality. "Have you guys looked at these walls? I mean, *really* looked? They're carved sandstone. Giant bricks, perfectly placed, row upon row for miles and miles. Just look at them. The lines are so tight that the light doesn't even shine through."

I wheeled closer to one of the walls and really looked. He was right. The labyrinth was beautiful – ornate and intricate. Up close, each stone looked like it had been individually hand-carved. The patterns on every brick were new and original. Trees, flowers, women dancing. Each brick held a different scene. It must have taken years, maybe even decades to complete just one mile of the labyrinth – and we didn't even know how big the whole thing was.

Trent had already made that connection. "We don't build stuff like this anymore. I mean look at the carvings!" He pointed toward an image of a woman wading in a fountain. It was beautiful: all curved lines and whirling designs. "But, here's the thing: it's not old, you know? It doesn't look like it's been around for thousands of years. You can still see the leaves on the carvings of the trees."

I stared at the lips of the woman who was dancing in the water. He was right. You could see the carved drops of water falling from her hair.

Trent touched the image carved into the stone. "It just makes me wonder if maybe we're not just in a different place. That's why I said the thing about the 21st century. I mean, what if we really are in a different when?"

"As long as it's still my birthday here," I said, and Maria laughed.

Trent groaned. "Whatever. Let's find your dad."

I let him drop it, but not because I thought he was nuts. To be honest, I was starting to think that maybe he was onto something. I mean, something seriously strange was going on.

There's no way there was a place like this that we had never heard about. A giant, hand-carved labyrinth? I'm sure it would have hit the news. I wouldn't have missed it online. Not with how much I read. Something would have come up.

But, honestly, I didn't want to keep talking about it to Trent. I needed to think it through first.

There were too many strange things going on. First, there was Prom with the key. The key that I couldn't seem to take my eyes off of. The key that felt perfect and warm against my chest. I could feel it nestled close to me just inside my shirt. Besides that, the door we had walked through – it had disappeared. And even though it was early evening when we left the party, the sun up on the hill looked like it had just come up. And, oh, yeah, we were in a labyrinth. A labyrinth that stretched farther than I could see.

Clearly, we weren't in Kansas anymore. Or the United States of America, for that matter. And possibly, we weren't even in the same century.

Trent went on ahead of us, head hanging a bit, obviously mad that we wouldn't listen to what he was saying.

But what did he want me to say anyway? I mean, yeah, you're right, it looks like we stepped back in time? Or stepped into a different world? That I had a key that could open a door straight into Ancient Greece? And we had left our world behind?

No way. Not possible.

Or was it?

I pulled the key out from underneath my shirt and rubbed its gentle curves. It sparkled in the white-hot sun.

Grandfather had known I had it underneath my shirt. He had told me to use it. And I did. Without a second thought. I wanted to help Dad.

But the door I had opened – it didn't lead into another room in his house. And Grandfather must have known that too. It opened up into this labyrinth. Miles and miles of carved sandstone walls in the hot desert sun.

How was that even possible?

I took one last look at the woman in the fountain, water dripping from her hair. She was beautiful, like some enchanting water nymph or fairy, but she also felt like she didn't belong there. She looked like she was trapped – like the walls were holding her in, forcing her to dance in that fountain until the sandstone wore away and the water ran dry.

I tore my eyes from her face and spun my wheels, trying to focus on the road ahead. I could see Trent further down the path, just at the edge of my sight. I sighed and started following him.

Maria fell into step beside me. "Stupid *chico*. I hate that he's here. Don't let him ruin your birthday."

I smiled weakly. She was right. I shouldn't let him ruin my birthday.

I mean, I didn't have any presents. Or candles. Or cake. But it was still my birthday.

She caught my smile and suddenly burst into song, her voice cracking on the high notes: "*Cumpleaños feliz, cumpleaños feliz, te deseamos todos, cumpleaños feliz!*"

She took an exaggerated bow at the end, and I applauded her enthusiastically. Then, with a puff of my cheeks, I blew out eleven imaginary candles. I could almost see the smoke lingering in the air.

Eleven years old.

Happy birthday to me.

CHAPTER FIVE

Turns out being in a labyrinth isn't as much fun as you'd think. It's kind of boring. Actually, it's really boring. Like, mind-numbingly boring. Like listening to Mr. Julian explain the relationship between a fraction and a decimal for the hundredth time. That boring.

I mean, it wouldn't have been so bad if it were just me and Maria there. But it wasn't. Trent was there too. As he kept reminding us.

Luckily, it wasn't just stupid New Trent. It was a little bit of Old Trent too. He was almost being normal. I might even say "nice."

Which was really weird. He was smiling even though he wasn't making fun of me, at least not as far as I could tell, and he hadn't called anyone a bad name in over two hours. Well, unless you counted purposefully saying Maria's name incorrectly and following it up with a list of famous Mariah's. Don't get me wrong – he was still super-annoying. That hadn't changed. But by the time the sky was turning darker, he just wasn't being as mean.

"You doing okay?" Trent asked.

See what I mean? Like that.

"Fine," I said.

"Not me," Maria kicked dirt right toward Trent.

"Didn't ask you, Ma-ri-ah," he said.

Well, maybe he *was* being a little mean.

"Well, I'm telling you anyway," she replied, grabbing her hair and yanking it back into a ponytail. "And anyone else who will listen. My stomach hurts, and I need to put some food in it. I'm hungry."

Trent winked at her. "I'm sure you are."

Maria's eyes darkened, and she asked him, "Are you hungry? I could shove my fist down your throat."

"Maria, please," I said.

"Yeah," Trent added. "Violence is not the answer."

Maria cracked her knuckles threateningly, but then she sighed and dropped her hands to her sides. "I know. Food is."

"We really do need some food," I said, feeling hollow inside and just too dang hot. "And water. I can almost feel my tonsils screaming for water."

"You don't have any tonsils," Maria said.

"I know! It's that bad. Geez, at least when I got my tonsils out, I got to eat ice cream all day."

Maria's eyes lit up. "We both did."

"Phish Food," I said, and we both started laughing.

Trent cleared his throat. "Um…what's with the fish?"

Maria's stomach grumbled. "We need to get some.

Preferably cooked. Fish sticks. With mustard."

"Gross," I said.

"So…how do we do it?" Trent asked.

"Drive thru?" Maria asked.

"Good plan," I said. "But I don't see a McDonald's nearby."

"How about Subway?" Maria asked. "After all this time in the hot sun, I wanna 'Eat Fresh.'"

I shook my head slowly. "We're a long way from a foot long."

Maria sighed. She knew it too.

I glanced over at Trent. He looked like I felt – exhausted. His brown hair was stuck to his forehead and he was covered in sweat. He slid down to the ground on the shady side of the path and reached into his backpack.

"Seriously, Trent?!" I said.

Maria let him have it. "Are you kidding me? You loser. You had those in your backpack the whole time? And you didn't even share them?"

Two Clif bars sat in his lap; their bright blue packaging stood out amid all the tan and brown. They looked…delicious. Chocolate chip and peanut butter. The perfect combo.

But it didn't look like Trent wanted to share.

"I didn't want to eat them right away," he said. "I didn't know when we would find food next. And I thought they would just make us more thirsty. And my water bottle is empty. I forgot to fill it up. I'm such an idiot. We should wait. Seriously. We need to get to one of those fountains."

Maria kicked sand at his feet. "We haven't eaten for

hours, and you're just hoarding them all to yourself? Hiding them in your backpack? Not eating them?" She smiled darkly. "I'll take them off your hands, pretty boy."

Trent laughed, suddenly and sharply. "Seriously, Maria. You think I wasn't going to share? That I was just gonna let you guys starve? What do you think I am, some kind of monster?"

"I wouldn't put it past you." Maria crossed her arms.

"Of course you wouldn't. You're so stupid lately." He grabbed one of the bars and threw it at her. "Take it."

Maria grabbed it in midair and then just stood there, staring at him. Even in the hot sun, I could feel the heat of that gaze. But it didn't last for long. After a moment, she ripped open the package and shoved the Clif bar in her mouth, eating half of it in one go.

"Maria!" I said. "Could you at least not choke yourself? We don't have a phone to call 911."

"And no one would pick it up on the other side anyway," Trent said.

I closed my eyes and listened to the crinkle of the wrapper. A phone. I really wished I had one. I had tried to get a phone for my birthday, but Dad said they were too expensive, and Mom couldn't figure out the point of them. She said I could talk to Maria at school. Or on our home phone. Or "on the lines."

I didn't correct her. No matter how much I told her the word was "online," she never got it right anyway. She's never even sent an email. Last week, she walked down to the school to remind me that I had a dentist appointment after class – instead of just calling the school. She's seriously living in the Stone Age. And the moment we walked into that labyrinth, we were too.

I tapped my finger against the handle of my chair. There might not be cell coverage, but could we pick up grandfather's WiFi? Would that work? Or were we really miles and centuries away from his mansion? I mentally imagined checking for a signal on my laptop. I shouldn't have left it in the car.

Someone nudged me, and my eyes shot open. "Want some?" Trent asked, holding the bar out to me. "It's chocolate."

I shook my head.

"And peanut butter?"

"Nah. Let's keep going and see if when can find some water first. I'm pretty thirsty."

"You're missing out," Maria said, licking her lips.

I rolled my eyes. "And you're going to be even more thirsty after that Clif Bar, *señorita*."

"*¿Qué?*" Maria asked. "Are you saying you don't want yours?"

Trent thrust the other bar in his pocket. "No way. You can't have hers too."

Maria turned on him. "What's your deal, *chumaco*? Why are you being so weird? You're hiding all the food. Being super nice to Charlie. You got a thing for her?"

I could feel the heat rise up my face. I knew I was blushing. "Shut-up, Maria. We're all just hot and thirsty. We need to find some water soon."

Maria threw her wrapper on the ground and glared at me silently, crossing her arms over her chest. I glared right back at her. I couldn't believe she had just asked Trent if he liked me.

Trent, of course, was oblivious. He stood up and pulled his backpack on, staring into the distance. "I should have brought my water bottle. Or at least looked to see how far it was to the fountain when we were up on the hill. Then we would have known what to expect. I can't believe I—"

"Oh, you shut-up, too," I said. "You didn't. None of us did. So that's that."

"It's not like it would have mattered anyway," Maria said, arms still crossed. "We still would have had to walk this far."

"Yeah," Trent said, "but at least we would have known what we were getting ourselves into."

I wiped the sweat from my neck with the back of my glove and gazed down the long sandy path. "Not knowing sucks." Trent caught my eye, and I turned away quickly.

"You guys are dragging me down," Maria said. "I'm gonna run ahead."

"Yeah, you are," Trent said.

"What does that even mean?" Maria asked, throwing her arms in the air. She spun away and took off down the path without looking back.

I totally understood why she was running. We'd been in that labyrinth for at least twelve hours already; I could have used a little alone time too.

Instead, I was wheeling along with Mr. Pottypants himself.

"Where's she off to?" Trent asked.

"It doesn't matter," I said. "There's only one path."

"As far as we know."

He caught my eye, and I paused for a moment, thinking about what Maria had just said. "What *is* going on with you?"

"What do you mean?" he said, eyes shifting back ahead.

"Why are you trying so hard? And why are you being so nice?"

He started walking faster, but I kept up, turning my wheels quickly. For several seconds, neither of us spoke. I thought he was just going to keep on ignoring me, but he answered suddenly.

"He asked me to," Trent said.

"Who?"

"Your dad."

"What?" I asked, feeling my cheeks go warm. "When?"

"At the party. While Maria was pigging out."

"Stop getting off-topic. What else did he say?"

"Nothing really. He just told me to keep an eye on you. To make sure you were okay."

"Seriously? At my party?"

"Yeah."

"That's just like Dad. He's always treating me like a baby."

Trent shook his head. "That's not fair, Charlie. He's not treating you like a baby. He's just trying to protect you."

"What's the difference? He never lets me do anything. He always acts like I need help. You've seen him."

"Well…I…you know, maybe you do need a little help sometimes."

I slammed my hand against my wheel. "It's a

wheelchair, Trent. Come on. It's not a stroller. I can do things on my own."

"I'm not saying you can't." Trent's face was bright red as he pushed his hair behind his ear. "But is it so bad to ask for some help sometimes?"

I ground my teeth really hard and forced my wheels forward.

"Come on, Charlie," he said, shuffling behind me. "Say something back. Don't just get mad."

That was hilarious coming from Trent. He's angry all the time. "It's fine, Trent. Just leave it alone. I'm not mad at you. I just need to talk to my dad. I mean, why was he asking you to watch out for me anyway? Don't you think that's a little weird with everything that's happened? Do you think he knew something was wrong?"

Trent thought for a moment, and then he nodded his head, and his brown hair fell back into his eyes. "I think so. He…he reminded me about when my dad left. Out of nowhere. It was…weird."

Trent looked away from me. I couldn't see his face, and I didn't have to. "And then it got weirder. Your dad started talking about what it means to be eleven. What it means to be a grown-up. He kept stopping and stumbling over his words. It was so awkward. I thought he was just trying to make a point about your birthday."

"Some birthday." I could see Maria running back toward us, her ponytail falling apart, her hair flying in the wind. She looked so happy. I tried to smile like she did, but it felt all wrong.

"I guess this is what it means to be eleven," I mumbled.

"Stuck in a maze?" Trent asked.

"Yep."

"Guys!" Maria said. "This labyrinth is amazing!"

"A-maze-ing," Trent repeated, and I laughed.

"What are you laughing at?" Maria asked.

"You're slow," Trent said, and then flashed by her. "Race ya!" he yelled over his shoulder.

I'm not sure if he was talking to me or Maria, but it didn't matter. We barreled after him, kicking up sand and dust and laughing into the wind.

I pumped my wheels and lowered my head and focused in. Usually I can hold my own against the two of them, but the road was super rocky. My wheels kicked up too much dust and they kept getting caught, slowing me down. I looked up, and saw that Maria and Trent were far ahead of me, almost past my sight. They were probably shoving each other and running as hard as they could, both of them refusing to lose.

I wasn't worried – I'd catch up to them eventually. And to be honest, I was kinda happy they were gone. I needed some time to think by myself – without Maria harping on Trent and without Trent acting all weird.

I slowed down my pace a bit and then stopped to pull a rock from between the spokes of my chair. My wheels were holding up fine, and I hoped they stayed that way, since I had left my extra tubes in the car. I could probably figure out something though. Dad had walked me through how to replace a flat at least twenty times, even though I told him I understood after the first time. He just never listens to me. Which is funny, considering how he always says how he is so worried about me.

Mom is in and out. Sometimes, she'll spend three hours talking about our family and our future with me, eating Rolos and drinking iced tea, but then, other times, well, she won't talk to me for weeks. When she is working on one of her "projects," she doesn't like to break away from the "mood of the piece," as she calls it. That means that if I ask her a question, she might yell at me in Swahili, stomp and throw onions, or quietly hand me a muffin.

Last week, when I asked her to sign my permission slip to the aquarium, she smacked her thigh and yodeled. For five minutes.

I signed it myself.

Who knows what she would be thinking by the time my party ended. I'd already been gone at least 12 hours. And I had no idea when I'd get back. If ever.

She couldn't just slap her thigh this time. She'd have to do something.

I mean, Dad was gone too.

I sighed and ran my fingers through my hair. Maybe she wouldn't do anything. Maybe she'd just turn it into another performance piece.

But not one of her solo pieces. She'd have all of her artsy friends with her this time. And she'd do it as a benefit. She'd probably even bring in Cordelia as a guest star. I could see the posters in my mind: "Missing husband. Missing daughter. One Eggplant. In Three Acts."

At least I'd make it onto the poster.

Maria thinks my parents are cool. She loves how Mom lets me wear whatever clothes I find and how my dad is never around to bother us. Maria says her moms are a lot more controlling. I say they're a lot more loving. What I don't say is that if my Mom did tell me what to wear, I'd wear it, and if Dad was around more often, I might even listen to what he says.

That's the thing. He's always acting like I'm a baby. Always acting like I need help. But he barely even knows who I am anymore. He missed my last Computer Club presentation, and couldn't even make it to the award ceremony where I won my new laptop. And he doesn't even know what my project was about.

He's never around, and because he isn't, he always makes someone babysit me. Even though I'm eleven. Grandfather, Maria's moms, even Grandfather's new gatekeeper – Jaiden – they've all been put on duty. So many people have been put on Charlie Watch over the last few months. I'm really reaching my breaking point.

And now Trent just clocked in too.

Figures.

My nose started to run, and I wiped it on my shoulder. I was getting really cold in my short sleeves. At least I had my gloves. Maybe the opera gloves were a good choice. At least they kept me warm. I should have brought my hoodie. I thought it wasn't supposed to get cold in a desert, right?

Turns out I was wrong.

When the sun went down, it got cold. Really cold. Like shivering cold. Chapped-lips cold. Frostbite cold. If I didn't need my hands on my wheels, I would have hidden my arms inside my shirt. But I couldn't. I needed to push my wheels. I needed to keep moving forward.

Otherwise, it was going to be a long, cold night.

Anxious to catch up with Trent and Maria, I pushed my wheels harder. Why had they gone so far ahead? Why didn't they wait for me?

I could feel myself getting whiny. And complainy. But I couldn't just act like I had a Yankee-Doodle Dandy attitude – another one of Dad's favorites – when I didn't.

I knew I needed to take that whole elephant one bite at a time, but the walls were pressing in, crowding out the last of the light. I was cold. I was lonely. I wanted a shower. And I wanted to be at home in my bed.

If anyone had told me that this would be how I was celebrating my eleventh birthday, I would have laughed in their face.

I wasn't laughing when it turned completely dark an hour later, and I still hadn't run into Maria and Trent.

I could barely see the walls on either side of me. The stars, those pinpricks of light, had disappeared behind a dark cloud that seemed to press down on me. And the walls kept sneaking up on me too. I'd think I was going straight and then one of my wheels would scrape along a wall, and I would have to readjust. If I went too fast, the dirt kicked up and the wind blew it back in my face. Plus, I was getting really cold. Even with my gloves on, my fingers were starting to get numb, and my nose wouldn't stop running. My ears were freezing too. Yankee-Fricking-Doodle.

Add to that the fact that I was super-thirsty. I hadn't had anything to drink since before the party. I had downed a Mountain Dew before we left – Maria had left it in the fridge – and man, did I need it. I didn't have the energy for that party. Of course, I didn't know I'd really need that energy for an endless labyrinth. Since that last drink, I'd been wheeling around in the hot sun all day. I was starting to feel lightheaded.

As far as I knew, Trent and Maria hadn't had anything to drink in a while either, and Maria had eaten the Clif Bar. And all that cheese.

Maybe that was why I hadn't seen them? They found some water and were waiting for me to come to them? They were probably splishing and splashing in a pool of effervescent delight.

I knew I was being stupid. But still, I was surprised they had run so far without me. And maybe I was getting a little angry. Why did they run so far ahead? I mean, seriously, where were they?

Okay…so, maybe I was little more than mad. Maybe – just maybe – I was getting a little scared too.

I felt a sudden flash of wooziness and stopped pushing my wheels to hold onto the handles of my wheelchair. The walls spun around me and settled around a flashing green light.

I rubbed my eyes, but it kept flickering in the distance. A pale, green flame. Just at the end of the path.

I should have been a little more freaked out – I mean, weird green flames? A labyrinth that was dark as midnight and so very quiet? But I felt a calmness roll though me as I wheeled down the path toward the flame. When I got closer, I watched the flame grow larger, pulsing and pushing outward, until it was half as big as me. Incredibly, it unfolded itself and pulled upright, resolving into the form of a man. A man I had seen before.

Prom.

CHAPTER SIX

"Hello, Charlie." His voice sounded like a record player or a bad speaker.

"Prom."

"You used the key." His eyes flashed green, and parts of his body flashed in and out of existence.

"Yes," I said, trying to focus on his shifting eyes. "I did. To find my dad. Where is he?"

His form shivered in front of me. "I have not seen him since your party – which was wonderful, by the way. I had a brief conversation with him about you, and then he went to speak with your grandfather."

I shook my head. "That's not – but – we talked to him. To Grandfather. He said Dad came through the door." I paused, for a second, replaying the conversation in my head. *Did* Grandfather say that?

"Sorry, Charlie, but you are unfortunately mistaken. Your father did not follow me here. But, if you'd like, I can help you find him?"

I felt this sudden pull inside me, this desire, to trust Prom. It was like a warm ball in my stomach, urging me toward him.

I stared at his hands, which were wrapped around a sparkling, golden staff. His nails were long and dark. The image of a snake slipped into my mind, and I slid back in my chair. He was just as creepy as before. I knew, deep down, that I shouldn't trust him. Grandfather didn't. And he must have a reason.

"No, that's okay. I'll find him on my own."

"Understood. It is your choice. But I will be here if you need me. Just ask and I will help you."

The warm ball spread through me again. Was Prom doing that? How was he doing that? "What's happening to me? I feel weird. Why is your staff glowing? And where are you? I don't understand. You're not right in front of me. How are you doing that?"

"Very perceptive, Charlie. I am at the castle at the end of the labyrinth. I had some…things…I needed to take care of."

"But how are you here? Are you some kind of hologram?"

His form shimmered in front of me, trailing green smoke. I lifted my hand and waved my fingers through the tail of his cloak. It dissolved into the night.

"You really are just like your Dad," Prom said.

I pulled my fingers back from his wavering form.

"He cannot accept the idea of magic, you know. He's always questioning what it is, where it comes from, and who can have it. He never just enjoys it."

I pushed my hair out of my face. I'm not sure how I felt about magic. I mean, up until I entered the labyrinth, I didn't even believe it existed. But with the cold desert wind on my face, and the walls sliding upward into the night, I don't think I could really question it.

I touched the key hanging around my neck. It felt warm against my chest. I held it between my fingers. "How do you know my Dad?"

"We're old friends. We go way back." He laughed a little at some inside joke. Whatever it was, it didn't seem very funny in the middle of the cold desert night. "I am exceedingly sorry I cannot help you find him. But I have come to offer you something else. Something more than that. I've come to offer you…well…everything."

My mind caught on the word. Everything. "What do you mean?"

"The key," he said. "I can show you what it can really do. The possibilities. Its unbelievable power. Your strength. Together, we can bend time and space—"

I grasped the key a little tighter. "Listen, I don't really think—"

"Charlie, please listen. You do not understand. With that key, we – you and I – we can change history. You traveled through time. To Ancient Greece. But you are fumbling through the darkness. Together, we can do so much more."

Ancient Greece. We had really traveled back in time. We used the key to open a door and—

It was as if my mind exploded outward. I suddenly

realized what he meant. The key – my key – had brought me back in time. It had brought me to a different place. With it, I could change the past. Which also meant I could change the future. I could rewrite history.

I could make things different. I could make things better.

What would I change? The Holocaust? We studied that last year. It was terrible. Horrible. Millions of people died. But I could go back and stop it. I could stop all those deaths. All those murders. I could stop the entire war.

I just needed someone to show me how.

Prom stretched his hand out toward me. "I can show you. How to do it. How to bend time and space. How to make the world a different…a *better* place."

The way he said *better* made me uncomfortable. It had felt good when I was thinking it, but when he said it, well, he made *better* sound like a disease, like something gross. I opened my mouth to say something, but, in a moment, that feeling disappeared. It was like my thoughts fell into a thick, heavy, warm fog. I couldn't make any sense of them, and I couldn't remember why what he had said sounded so wrong. Instead, my mind was drawn to his idea. My thoughts were pulled toward him like he was a lighthouse in the fog.

He was the light. He shined. With him, I could do it. *We* could. Together. We could make the world different. We could make it better. But I didn't know where to start. "I don't know—"

"You could learn," he interrupted. "Together, we could open so many doors"

"There are more doors?"

Prom's face flickered in front of me. "Did your dad teach you nothing? Of course there are."

Dad. My brain slid around the thought. My dad. I tumbled toward a memory. He was why I had entered the labyrinth in the first place. He was the reason I had opened that first door. He was gone. I had to find him.

I shook my head, trying to clear away the fogginess. It clung to me, like a virus, making my thinking slow and unclear. I focused in on the one thing I knew, the one thing I understood: I needed to find my dad. I needed to bring him home.

Dad…he needed me.

I sat up a little straighter in my wheelchair. I didn't need anyone's help. They needed mine.

I looked over at Prom. His orange eyes shifted in the darkness. Weren't they green a second ago? I shook my head and they were purple.

Everything was getting weird. I was woozy and needed some water. But Prom was looking at me very carefully, like he was waiting for something. I remembered that same intense look from outside Grandfather's front door.

"Thank you very much, Mr. Prom," I said. He tilted his head. "I really do appreciate the offer. But, I don't think I'll be needing your help. I'm doing fine. I just need to find my dad."

His face flickered, his eyes flashing green and orange again, and then a smile spread across his face. "Of course, Charlie. You must really be missing him. I truly wish I could do more. But please—" He lifted his staff and a green flame ignited on its tip. He held the staff to his other hand, and I watched as the flame resolved into a large golden cup – no – a water bottle. A Dasani water bottle.

What the heck?

"Take this," he said. "As a gift. An offering of help. Now, and in the future. Just call me if you need me."

Before I could ask him how to call, the water bottle fell into my lap, and he disappeared instantly, taking all of the light with him.

I stared at the outline of the water bottle in the darkness, feeling the trickle of condensation under my fingers, trying to decide what to do next.

I was pretty sure that water bottle fell into the realm of taking candy from a stranger. My dad had warned me thousands of times to not eat the Halloween candy from the creepy house, and to not get in a car if it wasn't him or Grandfather driving. But you can't imagine how thirsty I was – how deliriously thirsty. And the blue of the Dasani label seemed to almost glow in the darkness, like a promise.

I uncapped the lid and downed it.

When it was gone, I unconsciously looked for a recycling can, then realized what I was doing and laughed at myself. I went to set it down against the wall, and then changed my mind.

We could use it. Fill it up at the next fountain. I squeezed the bottle, and it crinkled under my fingers. I wasn't just hallucinating. I really had talked to Prom. And he had some crazy weird magic.

I tucked the bottle in between my leg and my chair. I'd show it to Maria and Trent later.

But what would I tell them? That he had offered to help me? To change the world? Make it different? Make it better? And it seemed like a pretty good idea?

I rubbed my hand slowly across my face. I hadn't thought about what the key meant until Prom had offered his help. Everything happened so fast. I was a jerk to Dad, took the key from Prom, found Grandfather on the floor of his study, and then crossed into this strange world. I had been so focused on finding my dad, or a way out, or just something to drink, that I hadn't even realized the power that hung around my neck.

I reached in the top of my shirt and pulled out the key again. It looked so simple. Beautiful, no doubt, but it didn't look like it was going to change the world. It didn't look like it could really do anything.

But I remembered how it had felt to slide the key in the lock. To pass through that door. To feel all that power charging through me. It had felt good. So good.

I smiled. Then I almost laughed. I could do it again. I could find more doors. More worlds. I could change history.

Where would I start? Sure, there was the Holocaust, but what about the Black Plague? The Trail of Tears? The Rwandan Genocide? Syria? What mattered most? And how could I make the world a better place? What would I have to do? The questions and the possibilities flew through my mind, spinning back and forth in a crazy jumble. I'd opened one door and stepped back through time. Did it work on every door? Or was it only specific doors? And were there things I couldn't change? Or shouldn't change?

I pounded my hand on the seat of my wheelchair. I needed someone to show me how to do it – how to even start.

Wait. Dad could! He knew about the key. Prom said so. He could show me how to go back! He—

He knew. Dad knew. All those years. He knew about the key. And he hadn't told me, hadn't prepared me, hadn't helped me.

He had never told me anything at all, and now he was gone.

And I was fumbling in the dark.

When I found him – not *if*, but *when* – I was going to lay into him. And Grandfather too. He was hiding something. He knew Prom too. But there was so much I didn't know. So much I wasn't prepared for.

I stared out into the dark night, following the line of the labyrinth into the distance. The quiet and the dark surrounded me, but I wasn't scared. It was like my mind was finally clear, like I could really see for the first time.

Once I found Dad, I'd use that key. I'd go back in time. I'd make the world a better place.

I straightened up in my chair and tucked my hair behind my ears. It was a long, dark night, but I could finally see where I was going.

Then, out of nowhere, I heard it. A trickle. Like the sound of a leaky faucet.

Water.

Of course I would find a fountain right then. After just taking a bottle of Dasani from a freaky guy. Wait – a freaky hologram. I had just talked to a hologram, and he'd dropped a bottle of water in my lap.

I really had been in the hot sun too long.

It was dark and hard to see, so I kept my ears trained as I wheeled forward. The trickle was getting louder now. The fountain was probably just around the bend.

I wheeled around the corner, and there was a deep shout. "No!"

"Trent?"

I couldn't see him. I couldn't see anything. But I *heard* something. A muffled sound and heavy breathing, a snort, and then, "ROAR!"

Something slammed into my wheelchair. I hurtled into the wall. I put my hands out in front of my face as my legs spun beneath me. My shoulder hit the wall, and I fell on top of my hands, and then they collapsed. I heard something shuffle toward me. I tried to flip myself over, but my legs were twisted underneath me. I took a deep breath and wrenched myself over, but then I felt it. Hot air on my face. Hot, wet, horrible-smelling air.

I looked up into the biggest pair of eyes I had ever seen.

And then I screamed.

CHAPTER SEVEN

The dark hairy face roared back at me, so I screamed again. Its head was bigger than my entire body. I reached out and punched it as hard as I could, but it was hard as a rock, and the punch only made it angrier. It grabbed me with one of its giant hands and held me up in the air.

"Are you with them?" it bellowed.

I stared at it. It was speaking to me. It was saying words I could understand! It pulled me in closer. I couldn't take my eyes off its gigantic horns. They were large and curved. And incredibly sharp. When I finally tore my eyes away from them, I found myself staring at teeth that were the size of my head.

"Are you deaf?" it asked, shaking me like a rag doll. My legs flapped freely, smacking into the beast.

That snapped me out of it.

"Excuse me?" I asked.

"I said are you deaf?"

"Obviously not!" I snapped. "And that's not a very nice thing to ask. Nor is it nice to flap me around like a piece of garbage. Set me down."

The monster's mouth hung open, then it closed its giant lips and snorted loudly. It looked between me and the sandy path, and then it suddenly let go of my shirt. I crashed to the ground, my legs twisted under me again.

I yelled in frustration.

It snorted again in response, but just kept staring at me with its huge brown eyes.

I gritted my teeth. "Could I get a little help please?"

It cocked its head, horns twisting to the side, then picked me up with one hand, pushed my legs out in front of me, and sat me down. I pulled off my gloves and ran my fingers over my legs, feeling for anything out of the ordinary. If I had been cut – or even if my legs had been broken – the only way I would know was if I felt it or saw it. I had to check to make sure I was okay.

"What is wrong with your legs?" it grumbled.

"Really?" I asked, almost screaming at the big hairy beast. "That's the first thing you say? After all of that? How about, 'Sorry I just dropped you' or 'I didn't mean to spit in your face.'"

It paused, then mumbled, "I did not mean to drop you."

"Okay," I replied.

"Are you with them?"

"Who?"

The night was still pretty dark, and I could barely see its face peering down into mine. It turned away and grabbed something. I heard a jostle, then a loud crack, and fire lit up the night. The beast's torch blinded me for a moment, and when my eyes finally adjusted, I realized things were much worse than I thought.

The labyrinth opened up into a giant courtyard, and right in the middle of it, Maria was hanging in a net over a large fountain. She was bright red and looked ready to explode. Beneath her, Trent was tied to a statue of a mermaid. Both of their mouths were covered and Trent's shirt was ripped. His eyes were bulging like he wanted to kill something.

When I turned back toward the monster, my breath caught in my throat. It was nearly fifteen feet tall, with brown hair covering its face and chest. It was wearing tattered grey pants and its hairy legs and hooves – the size of school desks – stuck out beneath them.

Its hair. Its horns. Its muzzle.

"You're a minotaur," I whispered.

"And you are a human. This is the last time I will ask. Are you with them?"

I nodded my head dumbly. It reached out its enormous hand to grab me again, but I raised my own hand and held it off. "Wait a minute. What'd they do?"

It snuffed and pointed up at Maria. "The girl one tried to drink the cursed waters. Then the boy one attacked me."

"I'm sure they didn't mean to make you angry."

Trent made a muffled sound. It didn't sound like agreement.

The minotaur was unfazed. "No one is allowed to drink from that fountain. No one."

"Good to know," I said. "And if we promise not to, will

you please let my friends go?" It felt weird calling Trent my friend again, but I figured I would do it if it meant he didn't get eaten by a minotaur. Or tied up and starved to death.

"I will let *her* go," it said, pointing up at Maria. "But the boy one stays. He tried to stab me with that." Maria's sword lay on the ground at Trent's feet; the blade sat on chunks of brown hair.

"Trent!" I chastised him.

He didn't look apologetic at all. He just stared me down.

I glared at him, trying to get him to understand. His eyes brightened, and then he cast them down. "Look how sorry he is," I said. "I bet he was just trying to help Maria."

The minotaur scratched its muzzle, looking back and forth between Maria and Trent, and then it sighed deeply. I heard a low grumble as it put the torch in a bracket on the wall near the fountain, but I smiled when it took the net down, with Maria in it.

At least the minotaur was a little bit reasonable. It held Maria in its hands as it freed her from the net. She sat still as it unwrapped the gag around her mouth, but once it was free, she reached up and slapped it. It didn't flinch, but Maria didn't either.

"Of course he was just trying to help me, you stupid *vaca*!" she yelled, shaking her fist. "You caught me in that weird trap, and then you were roaring around *como un idiota*, and how was he supposed to know you weren't some homicidal maniac who eats little *chicas* for dinner?"

The minotaur rubbed its snout and mumbled, "This one talks weird."

That *really* made Maria mad. "I talk weird? Really? And

this coming from a giant cow?"

"I am NOT a cow," the minotaur roared.

"Moo!" Maria yelled back.

The minotaur pawed the ground with one hoof.

I tried to grab its attention before it charged. "Do you like chocolate?"

"What?" it asked.

I pointed at Trent. "Untie him, and he'll give it to you."

The monster lowered its snout at me.

"Trust me," I replied. "It's worth it. It's like the best thing you'll ever eat."

"Better than the golden apples?"

I looked over at Trent, and he shrugged. "Definitely." I nodded my head deliberately. "Twenty times better. It's sweeter, and it melts in your mouth."

The minotaur stared down at Trent, and then back at me. "Give me this 'chocolate' first, then I will consider letting him go."

"No deal," Maria said. "Then you'll just eat the chocolate AND eat him. I don't want to see that. Even if he has been a big jerk lately."

"I am not going to eat him!" the minotaur roared. "Do not be disgusting."

"Then what do you have to lose?" I asked.

It held out its hand. "Show it to me first."

Maria walked over to Trent and reached into his pocket. She pulled the Clif Bar out and held it up in the air. She walked away from Trent, waving it around and crinkling the package invitingly. When she stopped, the sword was right in front of her feet. The minotaur didn't even notice.

Maria's smart like that sometimes.

"Deal," the minotaur said. "As long as *he* stays away from me."

The minotaur loosened Trent's gag, and Trent immediately responded, "With pleasure, big guy."

The minotaur untied Trent and stepped away as Trent walked over to Maria. The next few moments blurred by. Maria tossed the Clif Bar to the minotaur, and it caught it. As it began to open the package, Maria kicked the sword up into the air and into her hands (um…awesome?!) and Trent grabbed the rope. He ran around the minotaur in a circle, staying low. The minotaur tried to grab him, but Trent dodged out of the way. Looping around the minotaur twice, Trent yanked really hard, and the minotaur fell to the ground, its feet tangled in the rope. When it tried to get up, Maria held the sword to its throat.

"Don't even move," she said.

The minotaur roared, pounding its fists against the ground, but it stayed beneath Maria's sword, breathing heavy. Trent took the Clif Bar away from it and tossed it to me. Then he wrapped the rope around the minotaur's wrists and back around the mermaid statue. It didn't look like the rope would hold, but that didn't seem to matter. With the sword at its throat, and its hands tied back, the minotaur went limp and stared at the ground dejectedly. "And that is why you never trust humans," it said.

I slid my body closer, and Trent took a step forward. I waved him off as I examined the giant minotaur lying beside me. It blinked its cow eyes and wrinkled its wet nose. I noticed more than a spark of life in its brown eyes.

"What's your name?" I asked.

"Asterion."

CHAPTER EIGHT

"Asterion?" A flash of warmth broke through me. "Your name is Asterion?"

He blinked again slowly. "Yes."

"My grandfather, he sent me! He sent me to find you! He said I need to see you! Somebody took my dad! The automatons? And they hurt my grandfather! I'm supposed to find you!"

Asterion's giant eyebrows furrowed, so I tried to slow myself down. "My grandfather. Charles Kleis the 13th! Do you know him?"

His eyes brightened. "Of course I do. I have known him for years. He gave me so many books!" His bright eyes faded as he narrowed his eyes and really looked at me. There was an intensity, a seriousness in his gaze that made my stomach shift. "Who exactly are you?"

"Charlie Kleis the 15th."

"The 15th," he repeated, staring at me with those deep

brown eyes. "And your dad is Charles?"

I nodded my head.

He sighed, long and deep. "I should have known who you were. Your father was here yesterday—"

"Yesterday?" I asked. "But how? He was with me all day yesterday. We had therapy. And PT. We went to the Golden Garden for dinner."

He squinted down at me. "You do not know how the portal works yet, do you?"

"The portal?"

"The door. Did you cross through after he did?"

I nodded my head.

"Time works differently here. Your father passed this way yesterday. There was a battle—"

"A what?" I asked. "A battle?"

"A battle," Asterion said. "I did not win. But your father escaped. The last time I saw him, he was chasing after Prom. I would have followed him, but I had to deal with that." He pointed over at a pile of metal on the other side of the courtyard. "And then your friends attacked me."

Maria huffed. "We did not attack you. You attacked us."

"So says the girl with my hair on her sword—"

"Guys!" I yelled. "Seriously! What about my dad? And the battle?"

"Sorry," Asterion said. "It was Prom. Prom and his mindless minions."

Prom. He had told me he hadn't seen my dad. Told me he couldn't help me find him. But, really, he *had* seen him. In fact, he had done more than see him. He was literally battling him.

And I had just let Prom go.

Well, that wasn't exactly true either. I had just let his hologram go. I had refused his offer of help, but I had still taken his water bottle and just accepted everything he said. How could I be so naive? And stupid? "What happened?"

He stopped talking to Maria and stared down at his hands, which were still bound tightly together. "Ropes, please?"

I nodded at Trent to cut him loose.

Trent kicked the sandy path. "Do we *have* to untie him?"

"Just do it," I said.

Asterion laughed. "Ah, now I recognize that one. He is just like his father."

Trent's blue eyes darkened, and he ripped the rope tight around Asterion's neck. "Don't you ever say that. I am nothing like him. He's a monster."

Asterion shook his head as the rope pulled tighter round his neck. "You know nothing of him."

"And neither do you," Trent replied.

"Trent," I whispered. "Let him go."

Trent's face brightened, and his fists were white against the rope in his hands. I had never seen him so angry.

Maria touched his arm. "Come on," she said. She patted his arm and shook the rope loose from his hand. He let the rope go, and she began to untie Asterion. "I know everyone has a lot they want to talk about. You guys all *love* to talk. And I know we need to find out what happened with your dad. But we can talk while we walk. We need to find some more food." I smiled at her one-track mind. "Plus," she added, "if he's not gonna let us drink 'the cursed waters,' we're gonna need to find some water somewhere else."

Asterion sat up and pointed down the labyrinth. "We will go to my house. It is not far away. I have water there."

Trent scrunched up his face and started to say something nasty, but I raised my hand and cut him off. Grandfather trusted Asterion. And he had just fought beside Dad. We could trust him too. "That sounds like a good idea. I think we could all use a little rest. And I'm starting to get cold."

Trent looked down at me, and his expression softened.

I looked away toward Maria. "Can you help me to my chair?"

Trent reached down toward me. "I can—"

"Shut-up, *chumaco*," Maria said. "I got this."

Maria had helped me back into my chair a million times, so I wasn't worried. And Trent could have helped, but that just seemed too awkward. And I definitely didn't want Asterion lifting me up again anytime soon. His hands were like granite.

Maria walked over to me and squatted down, grabbing me around the waist firmly. She swung me up over her shoulder and then grunted as she straightened back up. Man, I'm lucky she's so strong. Even though I *am* stick thin, I'm so heavy. Not very many people can pick up a dead weight like me.

Maria shuffled over to my chair, which was still on its side. She sat me down next to it, exhaling as she set me on the ground, and turned toward the chair.

I glanced up at Asterion. "That's how you do it, you

know. Gently. You don't just drop somebody."

I could swear that underneath all that hair I saw him blush. I smiled up at him to lessen the sting. You can't just go around dropping people all the time.

"Um…Charlie?" Maria said.

I looked up at her. She wasn't looking at me. She was staring down at my chair. I grabbed my wheel and yanked on it to right it, but then I understood what she meant.

It was totally destroyed.

The wheels were bent so badly that they rested on the seat and there was no sign of the foot rests. It looked like it had been run over by a steamroller. Which didn't make any sense. It had just collided with a wall.

I felt like someone had punched me in the chest. All the time I had spent in that stupid chair. I covered my face with my hands. After my diagnosis – after the falls and the shakes and the dissolving muscles – after my legs stopped working, I had to wear braces and I had to relearn how to sit up. It suddenly took me so long to do these basic things, and there were so many other things I couldn't do anymore.

But once all that was over, once I was as good as they thought I could get, they sent me home from the hospital. But they didn't send me home in a good chair. They sent me home in a big, old, clunky chair that screeched whenever the wheels turned. They sent me home without my shoes – because nobody could find them and why would I need my shoes when my feet didn't even—

The chair. The chair. That very first chair was like a torture device. I got pressure sores in the weirdest places, and I even had to use two hands to turn a corner. It was awful.

Every six months after that, we rented a new chair. But they were always big and clunky like that first monster: hard to maneuver and uncomfortable after a long day at school.

Then on my tenth birthday, it arrived. The Quickie Zippie.

No birthday card, no note – just a big red bow.

Dad was so annoyed. He hated when Grandfather "pushed his money on us." He loaded the chair up in the car and drove over to Grandfather's house and tried to give it back to him, but Grandfather said he didn't know anything about it. Santa must have come early.

Still, he winked at me when dad packed it back in the car.

I loved every single moment in that chair. Racing down our ramp, flying after Maria, "accidentally" rolling over Trent's toes. It was like a part of me.

And now it was gone. Crushed by some crazy minotaur in a labyrinth in the middle of nowhere. And no-when.

My breath disappeared from my chest.

And then I got angry. Like, Hulk angry. If I could have gotten up, I would have run back across that courtyard and hit Asterion straight in the face.

Instead, I yelled. Really loud. Then I grabbed a rock on the ground beside me and threw it at him. Then I threw another. And another. They landed at his feet. Some of them knocked against his shins. He just stared at me. And so did Trent. And Maria. They all looked really sad.

After a while, it got kinda old. So I stopped.

I was still really mad. But like Mr. Julian says, sometimes you just have to enjoy your cookie.

So I did. I grabbed the Clif bar, ripped it open, and scarfed it down.

About halfway through, it got a little awkward. I mean, everybody else was just standing there watching me. I knew I was being weird, too. Mean. Petty. Selfish. I mean, it was supposed to be for Asterion. He'd never even had chocolate before.

But I didn't care. I swallowed it down. Finished it off. I didn't share, and it felt good.

"So," I said, shoving the wrapper in my jeans, "what do we do now?"

Turns out, not a lot.

We sat around while Asterion tried to bend the wheels back into shape. He grunted and flexed, but no matter what he did, they wouldn't roll right. And the seat was a mess. After a half hour, we finally gave it up as a lost cause.

I put my arm around Trent and Maria, and they pulled me up to stand. Trent's hand was warm on my back, and his smile was a little off. I tried to just stare straight ahead and concentrate on not losing my grip. I focused on ignoring where his arm touched mine, the feel of his fingers on my hip.

Okay, I wasn't very good at it.

Asterion held the torch in the air and walked in front of us. When he was a little ways ahead, Maria whispered, "He's a minotaur."

"I know!" Trent said.

"This is so epic!" Maria said.

I couldn't help but smile. She was kind of right. We were actually following a mythological creature brandishing a torch through a giant labyrinth on a heroic quest to rescue my dad.

But the longer I thought about it, the harder it was to keep the smile.

My dad. Who knew where he was? And what had happened to him? And how would we ever find him? The whole thing wasn't really that epic.

"Sorry, Charlie," Trent said. "I know you miss your dad."

"It's okay," I said. "We'll find him."

"And," Maria said, "you'll get something to drink soon. Then you'll feel better."

I was about to tell her about Prom, and the bottle of Dasani, but then I realized I didn't have it. The bottle. Where did I leave it?

"Geez, Maria," Trent said. "Do you ever think about anything besides food and water?"

Maria's arm stiffened around my waist. "I think about cracking your face, *chico*."

"And I think about cracking yours, *chica*," Trent replied.

"Guys!" I yelled. "How about nobody cracks anything and you two just shut-up and carry me?" When I finished talking, I realized that sounded pretty bossy, so I added, "Please?"

Maria laughed and waved her other hand in the air. "Yes, Your Highness. As you wish."

I rolled my eyes at her. I'm not sure she saw it, but I

didn't say anything because right then, Asterion turned around and looked directly at me. He opened his mouth to say something, then closed it and turned around and walked ahead down the path again.

Things got pretty quiet after that. I think we were all just exhausted.

Plus, Asterion kept looking back at us. He wasn't saying anything, but clearly something was up. Finally, after the fifth time, I asked him, "What?"

His muzzle revealed rows of flat teeth. I think he was trying to smile. "I could carry you."

I nodded, but not in agreement. "I know. But we're fine."

"No, you are not," he said. "You are all exhausted."

Trent puffed out his chest and disagreed. "I'm great. I could do this all night."

"I couldn't," Maria said.

I squeezed Maria's shoulder hard.

"Ai! Lay off it, *Princessa.* We've been dragging you around for the last half hour. If he wants to carry you, I say you let him."

"It's not your choice, Maria."

"It could be," she replied. A little bit of her sass was creeping in to her voice. I knew what she was going to say next. "If I stopped helping you."

And there it was.

After all our time together, when I finally really needed help, when I finally asked, she wasn't going to give it to me.

I wouldn't have thought Maria would be the one to give up first. I would have put my money on Trent. I looked over at her, and saw her stringy and damp hair falling out of her ponytail. She must have really been wiped out. We had all had a really long day already, and she had also ran a foot race against Trent that ended with her tied up in a net.

I opened my mouth to tell Asterion to carry me, but Trent spoke first.

"How much longer do we have?"

"It is just around the next corner," Asterion replied.

I looked down the labyrinth to the end of the line. It wasn't too far. "Just get me there, guys. We can figure out something else for next time."

Maria sighed, but pulled me a little bit closer.

I wasn't mad at her. Far from it. I held her tighter too.

CHAPTER NINE

"We are here," Asterion said.

"Where?" I asked.

He held the torch higher in the air, revealing a large door in the labyrinth.

"Oh," I said.

It was the first door we had seen in the labyrinth. In fact, beside the "cursed" courtyard, it was the first new thing we had seen in the labyrinth at all. And I had almost missed it in the darkness.

It was giant, as tall as Asterion, and ornately carved, with images of a bull rushing through a desert. But when I looked closer, I realized it wasn't a desert I was looking at. Other images were carved into the sandstone. It was a labyrinth like the one we were in. And the image of the bull...he was charging forward, but anyone could see that the path would get him nowhere. He'd get to the end and have to turn back around again.

The carvings were delicate and beautiful and deeply sad.

"Who carved these?" I ran my fingers along the smoothed edges of the charging bull.

"I did," Asterion said.

"*You* did?" Maria asked.

It really said something about how good the carvings were that Maria was asking. She ignores everything except food and sports. But her eyes were glued to that door.

Asterion nodded his head. The light flicked off his big brown eyes as he looked away. He obviously didn't want to talk about it, which made no sense to me. If I had carved that, you'd never hear the end of it. I'd talk your ear off about it. Nonstop. And you'd listen, too. It was that beautiful.

He started to open the door, but Maria stopped him. "You really carved all of this?"

"Yes." His hairy hand settled on the image of the bull rushing through the labyrinth. "This was one of my first carvings."

"You made more?" Maria asked.

"Of course."

"Can we see them?" she asked.

Asterion raised an immense eyebrow and gestured at the walls stretching out before us.

Maria's jaw dropped. "You mean you carved *all* of the walls?"

He nodded his head and Maria's eyes widened further.

Trent harrumphed. "Impossible. That's just not possible. Did you guys even see how many carvings there are? There's, like, millions. It would take decades – no, centuries to do that. He couldn't have done them all."

"Time," Asterion said, gently touching an image of a fountain, "works differently here. Let us just say I have been here…for a long time. Prom made sure of that."

He dug his hoof into the ground as the three of us stared at him.

"What happened?" I asked, feeling the weight of the key around my neck.

Asterion snorted, forcing a stream of air out of his nose. "He trapped me here. Me – an immortal. He left me to rage inside the walls of the labyrinth. Then he killed my father – the Cretan Bull. He took everything from me. Even my mother. He forced her to marry Minos, who held her prisoner in his castle right up until the day she died. I have been here since I was a little boy and Prom kidnapped me and trapped me here. I would kill him if I could get to him."

Was this really the same Prom who had given me the key? Who had offered me a bottle of water and the chance to change the world? Had he really battled Asterion and my dad? I mean, Prom was a little weird, but I didn't think he was, like, an epically heinous bad guy. I just thought he was a creeper.

Asterion shoved the door with all his might, and it slowly shifted inward. Before he walked through, he stopped, and turned back to look at me. His eyes were hard. "I know you gave him too much, girl. And now here you are. Which means you have the key. And you have a lot to fight for."

I wondered at his words as my friends carried me into

the dark room. How could he know about the key? I hadn't even shown him. And did Prom really do all those things? Was he that evil? And was Asterion actually that old?

He set the torch in a bracket by the door, and we entered a giant room. An enormous oak table and two large chairs filled the left side. There was a darkened door in the middle, and then on the other side, a large slab of granite, carved with tiny rosettes, formed the mantel of the fireplace. In front of the fireplace was a mound of blankets and pillows. I looked down at my feet and saw sandstone tiles spreading across the floor and forming a diamond in the center of the room.

All that was beautiful, but it paled in comparison to the books. The walls were covered in them. You literally couldn't even see the walls. The books absorbed every empty space and climbed toward the ceiling. Some stacks even curved precariously along the arched roof. It was like heaven. Only without Wi-Fi.

"You like books, Asterion?" Trent asked. I squeezed his shoulder hard, and he almost dropped me.

"It gets lonely out here," Asterion replied, missing Trent's snottiness – or choosing to ignore it. "Especially at night. I carve the walls until the light disappears, then I crawl inside and into a book. They make the nights go by faster."

I nodded my head, knowing exactly what he meant. Books did that for me too. They took me away to fantastic and strange places. They made everything different. And good.

"Why do you stay here?" Maria asked.

At the same time, I knew what Maria meant too. Asterion's home was nice, but if you didn't like books, or carving stones, or walking around endlessly, there really wasn't that much to do.

"That is a story for the morning. We have other matters to discuss right now, and plans to make. Let me bring you some water and some bread, and then we will make our plans."

"Bread?" Maria asked. "Like, real bread?"

"As far as I know, it is real," Asterion said.

Maria looked up at him. "Don't you, you know, eat people?"

Asterion laughed, a big belly laugh that came from somewhere down deep. After it quieted to a low rumble, he said, "You must have heard that from Icarus. Little punk. Trying to make me sound big and scary so people would think he was a real hero. He even told everyone that he killed me, the little fledgling.

"But really, I let him live. Ariadne convinced me. She was the smart one." He looked over at Trent. "Your mother reminds me of her. Such strength."

"How do you know her?" Trent asked.

"Your father and mother were here for a time," Asterion said, pulling out one of the chairs. "Studying. Fighting." Then he looked at me. "And your father was too."

"What happened to my father?" I asked as Maria and Trent set me down in the large wooden chair. My feet dangled off the edge. "And why was he chasing Prom? And what do you mean by 'battle'? And where did my dad go?"

"So many questions," Asterion said. "And I do not have many answers. Your father, as a Clockbreaker—"

"A Clockbreaker?" I asked. "What's that?"

"The one who holds the key."

"Wait. Dad was a Clockbreaker too?"

"Yes," Asterion said. "The key is passed down from parent to child."

"Seriously? Why didn't he tell me?"

Asterion poured us each a mug of water out of a clay pitcher. "He was forbidden to."

Maria and Trent took their mugs and sat down in front of the fire, immediately downing them. I clenched the wood of my chair, my mug untouched.

"Your father is unable to speak a word about it," Asterion continued. "He was denied the power of speech. He always told me that when he tried to discuss the key, or who he was, it was like his tongue stopped up and his mind went completely blank. He would emerge from a fog several minutes later. It used to drive your mother to madness."

"He still does that!" I remembered how he had just spaced out on the way to the party.

"It is part of the magic of the key. And the magic of who you are." He tore a loaf of bread in half and passed a bit to each of us.

"I will tell you more in the morning," he said, as I stuffed my mouth full of bread.

"Nuh-uh," I mumbled, chewing quickly. "Not going to bed." I swallowed. "I need to find him. I need to know he's okay. Where is he?"

Asterion sighed, his breath rushing across my face. "The last time I saw him, he was chasing Prom toward the castle. That was hours ago. The automatons kept coming, wave upon wave. I didn't know he had that many."

"What's an automaton?" Maria asked.

"We have to go after him," I said, stuffing more bread into my mouth. I wiped the crumbs from my hands and gestured to Trent. He jumped up. Maria stayed where she was.

I waved to Maria and tried to speak over the bread in my mouth: "Come on—"

"Are you kidding?" she asked. "It's the middle of the night. And no one's told me what an automaton is."

I swallowed hard. "It's a stupid robot. Who cares? We have to find my dad."

"We will not make any headway tonight," Asterion said. "You are all too tired, and the labyrinth is too dark."

Trent shifted on his feet. "We could bring torches—"

"I do not have enough oil, and they are far ahead of us by now. We may as well prepare ourselves. We will discuss this more—"

I shook my head. "No—"

"You are exhausted. Sleep first. Then we fight."

I stared at him for a moment, not understanding. "Fight?"

"Yes, fight. Have you not been listening? Prom has armies behind him. I have not made my way to the castle gates in a hundred years. He is strong, and you are blind. Everything here is more than it seems."

Maria laughed and shook her head slowly. "It's a giant

labyrinth. It already seems like more than it seems."

Asterion settled his large cow eyes on Maria, and she shoved more bread in her mouth. "What you need to know, and what Charlie needs to know, is that everything is more than it seems. Even you."

Maria stopped chewing. "Me?" she mumbled, her mouth full of food.

"Yes, you," he answered. She looked away, but he went on. "You too," he said to Trent, who was settling back into his seat and totally not looking at me either.

"What—" I began, but Asterion turned back to Maria.

"But you know that," he said. And she lifted her head to meet his eyes. "You can run fast, right?"

Maria nodded her head.

"But you can run even *faster*, right? Faster than a Gryphon? Or the Pegasus?"

Maria shrugged. "If they can run, I can probably run faster."

"Um, what?" I asked.

Something wasn't right. She had to be lying. If she could run, like, super-human-fast, like flying-horse-fast, she would have told me. After 5 years, she would have said *something*.

Maria turned and looked at me. "I can run faster," she said, a faint smile on her face. "A lot faster."

I thought of how we had whipped down the hallway on the way to Grandfather's study. I had almost forgotten about that. "Why didn't you tell me, dork?"

"I've tried to. It's just – I didn't want to seem like I was rubbing it in your face."

"Oh." My stomach twisted around the bread, and my throat dried up. I grabbed my mug and drank the water quickly. I could feel all their eyes on me, but I couldn't meet them.

My wheelchair – my legs – had never been an issue for Maria. That was what was so cool about her. She had been my best friend since kindergarten. And she always made everything seem so normal, no matter how much it sucked. Other people would try not to look at my legs, like they were afraid that was rude – to just look. Which is dumb. I mean, seriously, it's not rude to just look at someone. What's rude is *how* people look at you, or in my case, how they *don't* look.

But Maria never made the looking a thing. She'd look at me, laugh with me, hang out with me, talk to me, and I'd never feel like anything was missing.

But she had been holding back. She hadn't told me how fast she was because she didn't want to make me feel bad.

I tried not to let what I was thinking show on my face. I didn't want to have to deal with the idea that even my best friend couldn't be straight with me. Instead I asked, "Really? How fast are you?"

She looked at Asterion, then back at me, a smile slipping onto her face.

"Run over and get that jug." I pointed to the corner of the room.

"Which jug?" she asked.

"That one," I said, pointing at the jug again. When I looked, though, it was gone. I turned back toward Maria: "I thought there was—"

My mouth dropped open. The jug was sitting in her lap. I never even saw her move.

"How did you do that?" I asked, pointing at the clay jug. "I never even saw you get up. You were just sitting there the whole time!"

She smiled. "I'm not just fast. I'm *rapidisimo*."

Trent laughed. "Awesome, Maria! That's so cool!"

I couldn't help but smile. It was amazing. I mean, seriously! She just ran across the room when I blinked. "Do it again."

"Do what again?"

The jug had disappeared. I looked back in the corner of the room, and sure enough, it was back where it started.

"Awesome," I said.

"Sweet," Trent replied.

I cocked my head to the side and looked at Trent. "Did you know she could do that?"

He shook his head while Asterion tossed Maria another piece of bread. She scarfed it down as Asterion explained. "It is one of the skills of the Elite. Passed down throughout history. Josh, Trent's father, is the Elite—"

Trent said a word then that I'm really not supposed to say. Even when I'm in ancient Greece. It caught us all off guard. I'll just say he said, "jerk."

Asterion broke the silence that followed. "Trent, Josh is not what you think. He's an Elite—"

"I don't care what he is," Trent said. "That doesn't forgive what he did. He shouldn't have left her. And he shouldn't have hurt those kids."

"Kids?" I whispered.

"It was not his fault," Asterion said.

"What do you know?" Trent asked. "Were you there? Did you talk to him about it? Have you seen him?"

Asterion held Trent's glare, his horns reflecting the torchlight. "I have known your father since he was a boy. And his father before him. He would never—"

"Never what?" Trent said. His face was red and his fists were clenched. "Never hurt anyone? Never hide anything? Never walk away? Don't act like you know him. You have no idea."

His words hung in the air, unanswered.

I had no idea Trent's Dad was that bad. What had he done to make Trent so angry?

Asterion scraped a hoof across the tile floor, and Maria chewed on her bread quietly. Trent's brown hair had fallen into his eyes. He whipped it back.

"So…" I said, trying to change the subject, "What about you, Trent? Are you some kind of god?"

Asterion laughed. "Zeus be blessed, Trent is not a god. Far from it." Trent ran across the room, his fist pulling back, but Maria was suddenly in front of him.

"Knock it off," she said.

"Get out of my way," Trent said.

"Or what?" Maria asked.

"Leave him be," Asterion said. "He may be small, but he does have some skills."

"Like what?" Maria asked.

"I think he can tell you himself."

We all looked at Trent. He unclenched his fist slowly. Under his breath he mumbled, "I can fight."

"Ha!" Maria laughed and poked Trent in the chest. "Sure you can! You really beat up Asterion!"

Trent's face reddened, and he poked her back. "That doesn't count. The cow—"

"Minotaur," Asterion said.

Trent didn't look at him. "He wasn't playing fair! He tricked me!"

"Tricked you?" Maria said. "How? By being a giant cow?"

"Minotaur," Asterion interrupted again. They both ignored him.

"You heard what he did!" Trent yelled. "The way he yelled! And the pounding! It sounded like he was on the other side of the wall!"

"It sounded like he was beating the snot out of you. Just like I do every time," she added.

"I'm always taking it easy on you, loser. You ever heard of restraint?"

Maria flipped a hand toward him. "You obviously have."

Trent smacked her hand down. "You wanna go now, Correos? I guarantee you: I won't hold back."

Asterion grabbed Maria by the shirt collar and tossed her into the pile of blankets on the floor.

"Hey!" she yelled.

"Leave it be, Maria," he said. "Trent would definitely win. Trust me – he can fight. He almost beat me—"

"Almost," Maria emphasized.

Trent spat his words at her: "Shut your mouth."

"Or what?" Maria shifted to her knees.

"Or I'll shut it permanently."

Asterion stayed between them. "Trent, she does not need her mouth permanently shut. But I really would not mind if she at least closed it for a moment." Maria glared at him, then shoved another piece of bread in her mouth. Where did she find that bread? "Listen, Maria, I have been training for years. Centuries. He is only eleven."

"Eleven and a half," Trent said, cracking his knuckles.

"Right," Asterion said, shaking his head. "Eleven and a half. Leave it to the Elites to argue over age."

"These Elites," I said, trying to calm things down a bit, "how many of them are there?"

"Seven," Asterion said. "The sons and daughters of Hercules."

Maria laughed suddenly. "Wait. My grandpa? He is sooo not Hercules."

"Can you imagine?" I said. "Mr. Correos as Hercules? He'd be all, 'Blah blah blah, I'm going to complete my twelve trials now. Just let me put on some pants. And finish *Wheel of Fortune*.'"

"Bankrupt!" Maria yelled, then burst into giggles.

"You guys are such dorks," Trent said.

Maria shot him a glare, but most of the heat of it was already gone.

"That is not what I meant," Asterion said. "I was referring to your ancestors. Many centuries ago, the sons and daughters dedicated their lives to protecting the one who held the key. They made a sacred pact. Now, they are drawn to the key, for good or evil."

"Wait a minute," Trent said. "Good *or* evil?"

"Sadly, yes," Asterion replied. "Not all of Hercules sons and daughters believed that only one person should wield the key. Some of them believed the power should be shared. Or held by someone else. They fought for it, and died for it. Their children bear that same burden. They each must decide if they will serve the Clockbreaker, or if they will serve their own ends."

"Well," Trent said, "I wasn't planning on *serving* her."

"What does that mean?" I asked.

"Me neither," Maria added. "I have other plans for my life. No offense, Charlie."

"You're totally fine," I said, still trying to figure out what Trent meant. "How long have you guys known about this?"

"The Elite stuff?" Maria asked. "I didn't know any of that."

"But, how long have you had these powers?"

"About six months." Maria looked over at me, her smile disappearing. "I'm sorry I didn't tell you."

"Whatever," I said. "It's cool."

"But I'm still not going to serve you," Maria repeated, her face relaxed again.

"Understood."

I wasn't offended. Really. I mean, who would want their best friend "serving" them? That could get really awkward. I would rather just be friends.

But *real* friends. The kind who didn't hide stuff from each other.

"They do not serve you." Asterion tapped his hand on the rough wooden table. "They serve the *idea* of you. They serve the key."

"And what exactly," I asked, "*is* the key?"

"I guess we should have talked about that first." Asterion yawned, his giant mouth stretching open, revealing a row of large, flat teeth. I imagined how my head could fit neatly inside.

Watching him yawn was freaky. At the same time, it reminded me how tired I was. My body ached, my head felt tense and heavy, and even though my mind was racing, I couldn't stop myself from yawning too.

"Can we just talk about it in the morning?" Maria said, as she caught the yawn too. "*Estoy cansada.*"

"Me too." Trent walked over to the pile of blankets. He suddenly stopped himself and looked up at Asterion. "But we're not finished here, Asterion. I have some questions of my own." His words were stones, breaking and crashing into my ears. I wondered if I even wanted to hear his questions.

More than anything, I wished for the Old Trent back. The one who brought an extra peanut butter sandwich on field trips because he knew Mom would forget my lunch. The one who waited after school with me when Dad was late to pick me up again. The one who always picked me first in volleyball, even though I couldn't really move around the court. The one who wasn't so angry all the time.

Instead we got New Trent – mad, mad, mad. Always looking for a fight. Always angry. And the way he was looking at Asterion – he was on the edge of rage.

I was clearly not understanding something.

"Agreed," Asterion said. In contrast to Trent's,

Asterion's hairy face was blank and stiff. "Get some rest. We leave at first light."

I'd heard people say that in movies, but I'd never really been up that early before. Mom says anything before seven is gross. I'm with her on that. I hate getting up early.

But it would be okay this time. We had to get up early. Honestly, it was stupid we were even going to sleep.

In the back of my head, I knew we were all wiped out, and we'd be much better in the morning if we got a little sleep. But I doubted I would get any at all. Too much had happened that didn't make any sense. I was a Clockbreaker, my friends were epic heroes or something, and my dad was chasing a crazy hologram guy. I kept feeling like there was something I was missing.

"May I?" Asterion asked. He pointed toward the floor and I nodded. He lifted me with his giant hands and set me onto one of the blankets. I watched him as he fluffed a pillow awkwardly.

His left foot was as big as my whole leg. But, big as he was, he was trying to be gentle.

"I am sorry I broke your chair," he said quietly, pulling a blanket over my legs.

"It's okay," I said. "I'm sure Grandfather will buy me a new one."

Asterion smiled. "He would. He would do anything for you. The day you were born, he told me he laughed. A great, big, gut-shaking laugh. It frightened the nurse." His face softened. "They all thought you were going to be a boy. And when you came out, well, *you*, he thought your father was going to just die of shock. But Grandfather knew, we all knew, that you had your father wrapped around your finger the second you arrived. He would have done anything for you."

"But he still treats me like that little baby. He refuses to let me do anything. And it's just because I'm in some stupid wheelchair—"

"Charlie, it has nothing to do with that, and you know it. He has held you close since the day you came into this world. Your Grandfather told me that when you were first born, your father was scared to hold you. Afraid you would break. After your mother settled you into his arms, he wouldn't put you down. He was scared to let you crawl, to let you walk on your own. You were everything to him."

I remembered how it had felt to be carried in his arms. How his hands tucked underneath me and he pulled me close. One time we went to the zoo – I must have been five by then – and he never set me down. The entire five hours. I saw a zebra run by my legs from the top of his head. I got cotton candy in his hair. He didn't care. He always tried to take care of me.

But that still didn't take away my doubt. "But why," I asked, my voice breaking, "why did he call me Charles?" I dropped my head, my voice barely above a whisper. "He didn't even want me because I was a girl."

Asterion moved his giant hand and took my chin, pulling my face up to meet his eyes. "He wanted you before you were born. He named you Charles because he had to. To claim you. To give you the choice to bear the key. It can only go to a child who bears the same name as the Clockbreaker. If he had not named you Charles Kleis, the key would have been passed on to a different family."

"Wait…it hasn't always been in my family?"

"No. Daedalus created the key as a check on the power of the gods. Ares, the god of war, had been making a play for power. He was using humans as little pawns in his game. Daedalus gave the key to the line of Clockbreakers to protect it and to use it if the gods got out of control again. You are the fifteenth Kleis Clockbreaker. Fourteen Kleises came before you. The one before all of them was not a Kleis. He was a Schlüssel. Gerhardt Schlüssel the twentieth. The last of his line. After him, the key moved on to Charles Kleis the first."

"I don't understand."

"The Schlüssel line ended," he explained. "There was no heir. If you do not have a child either, or if you do not name him or her Charles Kleis, the key will move on again, too."

I thought about what that meant. What that *really* meant.

You see – the doctors aren't sure if I will be able to ever have children when I grow up. I might actually *have* to be the last Charles Kleis. Which means…I'll be the last Kleis to hold the key, too.

"Do not worry," Asterion said. "That is a long way off. For now, you have the key, and we have to get your father."

I nodded my head slowly, trying to take everything in. I was named after Dad so I could have the key after him…but why had he let me take the key in the first place? Why did he even—

The key. My shoulders loosened and I smiled. It didn't matter if we saved Dad at all. We just needed to get back home. Open another door. Travel back in time. And save him then.

"Why are you smiling?" Asterion asked.

"It's easy. It makes it all so easy. Don't you get it? It doesn't matter what we do here, or how bad I messed things up with Dad. We can do it all over again. We can even stop me from taking the key in the first place."

Asterion lifted one large cow eyebrow. "The Moirai are not so easily dismissed."

"The Moirai?"

"The Fates. They spun the thread of your life. For many years, they have woven the threads of humans loosely. You, however, your family, and your friends—" he pointed over at Trent and Maria, who were whispering by the fire. They didn't look up. "Your threads are woven more tightly."

"Meaning?"

"Your destiny has been decided."

I pursed my lips. "Oh, I don't believe that. I'm pretty sure we make our own destiny, that we make our own choices."

Asterion snorted. "It often seems that way. It is hard to see your path when you are so busy following it. You can believe what you want – but that does not change the reality."

I tried to think of something to say back to him, but I wasn't really sure how it all worked, and I wasn't thinking straight anymore. There were too many possibilities, too many mistakes. I tightened my fingers around my blanket as Asterion stood up, his hairy face lost in the shadows.

A final thought flew through my mind, and I grabbed his hoof. "You know so much. How? How do you know my dad? I mean, if he has the key, why are you still trapped in the labyrinth? Why are you here if he knows a way out?"

"That way is shut to me. Prom cursed it so only humans can pass through that portal. I will never leave that way."

So many years wandering the labyrinth. No end in sight. No real purpose besides guarding some fountain and carving rocks and reading dusty old books. Watching other people change history. All because of some stupid, creepy guy.

"Is he really that bad?" I asked. "Prom?"

Asterion looked directly into my eyes. "He gave you the water bottle, yes?"

Blood rushed to my face. Asterion must have seen the bottle. He must have known the whole time. "Yes," I replied.

"What did he offer you in return, Charlie? Did he offer power? Glory?"

I remembered how he had held out his hand. How he'd said we'd change the world. Make it different. Make it better.

"He said we'd change the world," I whispered.

"His words are ash," Asterion whispered. "His gifts are cinders. They flow like the cursed waters, but will never quench your thirst."

He stood up then, slowly raising his gigantic form and turning away from me.

I watched him go, but didn't want him to leave. There was so much more I needed to know. "Why were you guarding the cursed waters?" I said to his back.

He stopped mid-stride, his hoof digging a groove in the tile floor. He paused for so long, I thought he had decided to not answer me. But his voice came out soft and sad. "It is where she died."

"Who?"

"My sister. Ariadne." He shook his head slowly as her name lingered in the air around us. "No more stories."

He raised the torch and lit a candle on the wall, then whispered, "Good night, little warriors."

The light of the torch followed him into the other room, his shadow growing long behind him.

As the light faded, I knew I would never get to sleep. I turned to look at Maria, but she was already snoring, snuggled up under her blanket beside the fire.

Trent had found a spot on the other side of the fireplace. I could just barely make out his eyes. They were closed. I didn't think he was asleep though.

I rubbed my eyes and ran my fingers through my hair. The day had lasted forever – my longest birthday yet. And tomorrow would be just as long. I wondered if Asterion knew how long it would take us to get out of the labyrinth, and if we even could, and then I yawned two more times – really big stretchy yawns – and before I knew it, I was sound asleep.

I wheeled along the narrow path, jagged rocks looming above me. The air, dark and smoky, filled my lungs, and I coughed, chest heaving again and again.

My breath wheezed through my throat, and I pushed ahead, shoving my wheels forward. I had to find my dad. Had to save him from the—

Hot air blasted against my back. I turned and a wall of flame shot toward me, incinerating every rock and stone in its path. The flames seemed almost human: fiery hands reached out and sharp teeth destroyed everything in sight.

The flames reached for my wheels, and I shot forward into the night, the path – somehow – pitch dark and full of writhing shadows. I tried to wheel faster, but my wheel snagged and spun and suddenly, I was facing the flames again. I tried to wheel away from the fiery inferno, but I was too late. The heat cut into my legs. I closed my eyes against the fire on my face. The bite of the flames. This was it. My final moment.

I felt a hand tighten around mine, and I looked up at a shadow above me. The shadows brightened in the light of the flames.

"Dad!" I screamed.

He squeezed my hand twice, then let it go. He threw his glasses to the ground and pulled out a shining silver sword. With a guttural scream of defiance, he jumped into the flames.

"No!" I screamed. And the world went dark.

CHAPTER TEN

"What's wrong?"

I opened my eyes and Maria was looking down at me. I could still feel the heat of the fire on my chest, burning me. I rubbed my hand along my neckline, wincing as the key sizzled against my skin.

"The key!" I yelled. I tried to pull it off – to break the silver chain – but it wouldn't come free.

Trent jumped to his feet. "What's wrong?"

"The key! It's on fire! I can't get it off!"

Suddenly, the door flew open.

Maria ripped out her sword and had it at the intruder's throat in a second.

It was Asterion.

"How did you—" Maria started, but he interrupted her.

"Automatons!" he yelled. "Up! Now!"

"Automatons?" Maria asked.

Asterion pushed his way past Maria, batting her sword

out of the way with a flick of his finger.

"Will somebody just tell me what an automaton is?" she yelled.

Asterion ignored her and opened a dark wooden door in the back of the room. Its hinges creaked loudly. He rustled around in its contents, pulled out a small dagger, and held it out toward Trent.

"Are you kidding me?" Trent asked, glaring at the dagger.

Asterion rolled his eyes and shoved the dagger in his belt. He reached further into the closet, and this time he pulled out an ax.

Trent grinned and grabbed it from his hand. He swung it around himself in a circle. "Now *that's* what I'm talking about!"

Asterion knelt down beside me and looked into my eyes. "Will you let me carry you?"

I swallowed quickly and nodded my head.

"I might need to fight," he said. "How strong are you? Can you hold yourself up?"

I nodded. "But not forever." I looked around the room, then pointed at the blankets. "Grab that blanket and tie it around your horns. I can sit in it."

"Good thinking," Asterion said as he ripped the blanket in half. He tied it in a circle and then looped it around his horns. He picked me up and settled me into it. I grabbed a hold of the base of his horns, careful not to touch the tips. They looked wicked sharp.

And his hair – so sharp and wiry. It was not going to be a comfortable ride.

"Ready?" he asked.

"Ready," I said.

"Ready," Trent said.

"Vámanos," Maria said.

"Follow me." Asterion reached his hand inside the closet and pulled out a giant mallet. It was as tall as the door and thick as a tree trunk. It had to weigh at least a hundred pounds. Asterion wrapped his hands around its well-worn handle and lifted it with almost no effort.

Maria smiled, and Trent took a step back in awe.

"Yeah, um, Asterion's strong," Maria said.

"Which way are we going?" Trent asked.

"To the left," Asterion replied. "Beware. I sighted them three leagues ahead. We need to make it to the next courtyard so we can launch our attack. We only have one way we can go, but the automatons are not limited by the labyrinth. They love to crash through walls."

"Awesome," Maria mumbled, tightening her grip on her sword.

I held onto Asterion's horns tightly as we went through the door. Fifteen feet in the air is higher than you think.

The key started to burn again, and I tightened my jaw. "What's wrong with this thing?"

"Is it the key?" Asterion asked.

"Yes! It's super-hot!"

"It senses Prom's minions. Before Daedalus created the labyrinth, he worked with Hephaestus. They created these automatons to protect the key, but Prom did something to them. Now they work for him."

"Quiet down, both of you," Trent whispered from

behind us.

"It does not matter," Asterion said loudly. "If they are here, they will find us. They are drawn to the key, like flies on a pig."

"Are you calling me a pig?" I asked.

Suddenly, the wall in front of us exploded. Dust filled the air, and I coughed, hiding my face in Asterion's wiry hair. When I looked back up, the dust was hanging in the air around the base of the wall. There was a giant hole, but I didn't see anything on the other side. I held on as Asterion leapt over the rubble on our side and turned around, so we had the hole in the wall surrounded.

Seconds passed, and nothing moved. Just when I thought nothing was going to happen, a shimmery thing sprang through the wall. Its metal pincers scraped on the ground, almost like a spider, but it had the head and arms of a human.

It pounced on Asterion in a flurry of golden arms and razor-sharp legs. Asterion fended it off easily with his mallet; in one mighty swing, he sent it crashing into the wall. A black puff of smoke erupted from its caved-in chest, and then it collapsed. Its red eyes blinked twice, then faded out. One down.

Two more jumped through the haze, and I realized they moved in fits and spurts. Both of them spun around and looked at me. Their legs sprang to life – like some kind of weird spider-centaurs. Trent leapt directly behind one and swung his ax. The blow landed in a mess of gears and springs. At the same time, Maria disappeared for a moment and then reappeared in front of the other automaton, with her sword in its eye. Its legs collapsed inwards, and smoke poured from the pile of wreckage. Three down.

We didn't get a chance to catch our breath. Several more crawled through the wall. They were fast, but Maria and Trent were faster. And even though Asterion was a bit slower, he seemed to know what they were going to do before they did it. I wondered how long he had been fighting them.

I never thought I'd be in a battle with a bunch of robots. And even if I had imagined it in some crazy dream, I never would have thought it would be so…well…easy. Trent and Maria were dispatching automatons left and right, and Asterion had taken to stomping on them with his giant hooves. Still, they kept on coming through the hole in the wall.

"How many of them *are* there?" I asked Asterion.

"Who knows? There have been hundreds of them lately. The battle with your father was the most I have seen yet. I have been fighting them for centuries." He reached down and clubbed one into the wall, where it crumpled into a sparkling heap. "I do not know how Prom does it. He seems to have an unlimited supply of them."

Trent held up a severed, twitching arm. "Is this gold?"

"Yes," Asterion replied, before swinging his mallet into another one. The automaton flew toward Trent, and he whacked it with the severed arm, then fell on it with his ax.

He seemed to be really enjoying himself. He jumped up and began practicing what looked like ax-fencing with them. He led them along the edge of the wall, letting them repeatedly attack him while he blocked their blows with his ax. When he would get bored with one, he would whistle to Maria, who would run in and stab it in a series of quick bursts. The robot would fall, they'd high-five, and Maria would sprint away again. She seemed to be enjoying herself too.

They're so weird.

Honestly, it all just seemed kind of dumb to me. I mean, why waste all those automatons? Sending them in one after another to be shut down and destroyed… couldn't Prom do some decent reprogramming? I mean, it just took me my laptop and a lazy Sunday afternoon to hack into Wal-Mart and remove their pink Legos from inventory. Reprogramming ancient automatons *had* to be easier than that. In fact…

"Hey, Asterion."

"Yes?" he asked, whacking another automaton into a wall, where Maria quickly finished it off.

"Can you set me down on the ground behind you? I want to see what I can do with that automaton."

Asterion looked at the automaton he had sent sprawling, then spun around to whack another one in the face. "That does not sound like a wise idea. What if one gets through?"

"Are you kidding? That's not even possible. You guys are totally fine!" I yelled to Maria, "Aren't you, Maria?"

She disappeared and reappeared in front of Asterion a second later. "Totally. We got this *fiesta*." She turned around and hit an incoming automaton in the air with the hilt of her sword. It fell backward and Trent roundhouse kicked it in the head. Its eyes dimmed, and it collapsed.

Asterion backed away from the hole in the wall and lifted me up in one giant hand, setting me down gently next to the automaton. "When their eyes go out," he said, "well, I have never seen them come back on again. I just have to sweep them out of the way. You should see the pile of gold I have in the other courtyard. But still – be careful."

"Gotcha," I mumbled, staring at the golden body beside me. Eight spider legs sprouted from its torso, but it also had the upper body, arms, and head of a human.

It was eerie. The automatons moved so quickly when they were alive – was that the right word? – but the automaton beside me wasn't moving at all. Its eyes, which normally flashed bright red, were dark, like the bulbs had gone out.

I thought about the problem a little bit. No lights. Maybe the automaton had no power? If I wanted to get its system up and running again, I would have to repair the disconnect – make it a compete circuit. In this case, I would have to reattach the rest of its head. I looked at the wires and tubes protruding from its neck. I definitely did not have the right tools for that.

But, since its head was already partially knocked open, I did have the perfect opportunity to look inside and see how the automatons worked.

I touched its head and pulled my fingers back immediately. The automaton was wicked hot. The key around my neck suddenly got even hotter, and I pulled it away from my chest, swinging it away from the automaton. The key pulsed hard, and suddenly the automaton's eyes flashed bright red.

"Asterion!" I yelled.

The automaton opened its mouth. Asterion turned and raised his gigantic hoof.

"Master?" the automaton asked.

"Wait!" I yelled.

Asterion paused for a moment, leg in mid-air, and then placed his hoof on the automaton's chest, holding it down while it struggled weakly beneath him.

I looked into its flashing red eyes. "What did you say?"

"Master," it replied. "I serve the Clockbreaker."

"You serve the Clockbreaker?" I asked, staring down into its bright red eyes.

"Yes." Its clipped, artificial voice seemed to be coming from just below its mouth. "Daedalus created us to protect and serve the Clockbreaker."

Asterion snorted and pointed at Trent. I watched as Trent slammed another automaton into the wall, then quickly dispatched it with a swing of his ax.

Trent was incredible. I had no idea he could fight that well. Before we stepped into the labyrinth, I didn't know he could really fight at all. Now his arms were flexing, raising that ax, and his blue eyes were gleaming and—

I shook my head and tried to focus on the problem at hand. Asterion was right. Clearly something wasn't right here. The other automatons were attacking us. No matter what this automaton said, they were obviously not trying to protect me.

"If you are here to protect me, why are you trying to attack me and my friends?"

The automaton paused a moment as if it were thinking.

"My programming," it finally replied. "Someone has changed my parameters. We have now been ordered to destroy the Clockbreaker."

"So…why aren't you killing me right now?"

"It is a failsafe. Daedalus designed a hard-wired default automaton logic."

Asterion's muzzle twitched as he leaned in, denting the automaton's chest with his hoof. "What does that mean?"

The automaton's head buzzed and spurted. "In the event of a catastrophic failure, all automatons revert to their original programming if the key prompts them."

Asterion stomped down hard. "Speak regular words!"

"The key fixed me."

I smiled. Daedalus was brilliant. He programmed the automatons so they could basically be rebooted by the key. Like turning the power switch on my iPod off and on again when it was frozen.

Which meant…I ran my eyes over the broken automatons and smiled. I could use the key to reboot them all. We could make them follow our orders instead. They wouldn't try to kill us anymore. They would be fighting for us.

I looked at the piles of automatons around the hole in the wall and the growing number of bodies near Trent's feet. If we did it right, we could have a whole army at our disposal.

I explained my plan to Asterion. At first, he looked confused, then he looked skeptical, but by the end, his large brown eyes were gleaming.

"An army," he whispered. "At last. After all these years,

I can finally make it into Minos' castle."

"Minos?" I asked. He nodded, but instead of telling me what he meant, he turned around and barked the plan to Trent and Maria. They continued dispatching automatons, and he began to drag the broken bodies over to me.

"And guys," I added, "don't decapitate so many of them. You just need to incapacitate them so I can get near them and reboot them. We want them to be able to fight."

Trent looked momentarily annoyed, but Maria made it a challenge.

"First one to thirty with minimal damage wins," she said.

"Wins what?" he asked.

"The sword."

Trent sprang into action, like he had been holding back. He was a completely different fighter. Totally amazing. Like, unreal. The automatons never even laid a hand on him. And he didn't have to deflect any more of their blows. He dispatched them before they could even raise an arm or razor leg.

"I think he's going to win," I said to no one in particular. I wouldn't normally bet against Maria – she's my best friend – but watching Trent dance through the air, I knew it would be stupid to bet against him.

"Do not dismiss the girl," Asterion said. "She's moving so fast, you cannot even see her."

I watched two automatons mysteriously fall down with sword marks in their chests. He was right. I hadn't even seen Maria attack.

One by one, Asterion brought broken bodies to me.

The second they came near me, their red eyes started blinking, and they all said the same thing: "Master?" I ordered them to help repair each other while Trent and Maria kept adding to their number.

I turned to the first automaton I had revived. It had used its pincer hands to *mostly* reattach its head. "Do you have a name?"

Its face was cocked to the side, its expression strangely human. It righted its head and answered: "I have no name, Master. I am only here to serve."

"Can I call you Number One?"

Its eyes brightened for a moment. "Yes, Master."

"Okay, Number One. And please, no 'Master.' It's Charlie. Just Charlie." I pointed to Asterion, then to Maria and Trent. "That's Asterion, Maria, and Trent. They're my friends. Do you think you can help us?"

"Automatons are created to serve."

"Great! Thank you. I think we can actually do this." I smiled at Number One, and it nodded its head cleanly as I sent it off to work. It began clearing the battlefield as Trent, Maria, and Asterion pushed back the assault.

20, 30, 40 automatons. We were building our own army, but we had scattered, broken parts piling up too.

"This one is not functional," Number One said, dropping a busted automaton at my feet. Its head was missing, and its arm was broken. "What should we do with it?"

I stared at the spot where its head should have been, straight through to another automaton who was missing a leg. "We can use it for parts. Do you think—"

Number One sliced its pincer through the air and cut through the leg like chocolate.

"Apparently you can," I said, reminding myself to avoid those pincers and not shake hands with an automaton.

Number One skittered off to fix the broken leg, and Maria and Trent dragged even more automatons to me. I reprogrammed them, but at the same time, we couldn't keep up with that pile of broken parts.

So when Number One tossed another broken hand on the pile, I had an idea.

"Number One, how do your pincers slice? Are they heated?"

"Charged water is continually cycled through my boiler and available to all systems."

"Do you think we could make me a chair? Like melt down the parts to a seat with wheels?"

"Clarify your design."

I sketched a rough outline in the sand, explaining how the four wheels would need to rotate freely. I didn't go all out – I just went for functional – and kept my fingers crossed. Number One got to work, and I shifted between Number One and our new recruits.

I'm not going to lie. It was disgusting. I mean, they weren't alive, but it felt a bit gruesome to turn all those golden body parts into a wheelchair.

When Number One attached actual arms for the arm rests, I drew the line. "Could you…I'm sorry. Could you melt those down a bit? So they look like more this?"

I drew a rectangle in the sand. Number One clipped away, shaving off the fingers and reforming the golden wrists. I looked away again.

When I looked back, the chair was complete.

And I could already hear Trent laughing.

"That's a throne, Kleis!"

"Twenty-five!" Maria yelled.

"Did they make you a crown too?"

"Twenty-seven, *Princessa*!"

I squinted at the golden chair. It was wicked cool, but it was a little much. Luckily, I wasn't planning on rolling around school or anything. I just needed to make it through the labyrinth.

"Thanks, Number One. Can you put me in?"

Number One lifted me up and set me in the golden wheelchair.

The second my legs touched the golden seat, a jolt ran through me. "What—" A second jolt shook my thighs, and I choked on my words. The power ran up my legs and straight into my chest. My heart beat wildly, and my hands shook, and then, with one last jerk, it cleared my neck and swam out my mouth.

My body fell back into the chair.

"How is your health?" Number One asked. Somehow it was standing right in front of me.

"Fine," I said, wiping my hand across my face. "I'm fine. What was that?"

"For three seconds, I could locate your presence inside my matrix, as I do the other automatons. It must be the chair. It is complete now."

"The chair. Right. Maybe this isn't such a good idea."

Number One clicked its pincers. "Does it not satisfy

your expectations? We can rework the design."

"No. I mean yes. It's great. It's fine. But what if—"

"Does the gold not match your needs? We could find another material."

"The gold is fine. It's totally fine. The gold is—" And then I started laughing. It was so stupid ridiculous. An entire wheelchair, made of real gold, created by an automaton. And I was complaining about a little shock? I would be fine. As long as it didn't shock me again, I could survive the shining, golden chair.

Mom didn't even have a gold wedding ring. Well, she had one once. Then she lost it, and Dad bought her another one. When she lost that one too, he bought her a set of fashion rings from Claire's. Every other month.

Now, I had enough to supply her for the next century.

I reached down to turn the wheels, grasping onto the slippery circle, and then I remembered – the chair was solid gold. And heavy as…solid gold.

I resisted the urge to complain about my billion-dollar wheelchair. Somebody was going to have to push me.

And the cool thing was, we had a whole army of somebodies.

I caught Maria's eye as she clocked another automaton from behind. She smiled, and I smiled back. We'd have a whole army to keep her and Trent safe too. We could make this work.

As the battle died down, Asterion made his way back to me. "This will be more than enough." His cow eyes shined in anticipation.

"Now we just need a plan. Number One, we are trying

to get to—" I stopped. I didn't really know where we were going.

Asterion pointed a hairy hand into the distance. "The castle."

"That's where my Dad is?"

Asterion paused for a moment. "That is where Prom is."

"Then I guess that's where we need to go," I said to Number One. "Is that where you came from? The castle? How did you get here?"

"The door. Four thousand paces away. It is a portal. But it does not require a key."

"Wait, what's going on? Portal? Like the video game?" Trent asked, stopping beside me, holding an automaton out at arm's length.

Number One looked directly at him. "The portal is not a game. Minos forced Daedalus to create this portal so Daedalus could move back to the castle quickly when he was needed. It opens for ten minutes every ten days at ten in the morning."

Asterion slammed his fist into the ground, and the walls shook around us. Number One dove in front of me, pincers raised. I waved him off, but he refused to move.

"That is how they do it!" Asterion yelled. "Every battle, I am always overwhelmed by the sheer number of them. And I either retreat or wake up back at my house. Then I have to travel for sixty more days back to that ridiculous castle. And all they have to do is walk through a door!" His eyes bulged beneath his hairy brow, and he glared at Number One, who was still crouched down in front of me protectively. I nudged him out of the way. He moved slowly to the side, but stayed close by, pincers snipping the air.

"Let it be, Asterion," I said. "We know how they're doing it now. We'll be there in no time."

His brow unfurrowed and his eyes gleamed wildly. "And the Fire-eater will not even know we are coming this time. With an army." He looked over at Number One. "Automaton, where is this door?"

"His name is Number One," I said.

"On the other side of the wall," Number One responded.

We were so close to Dad. It was going to be so easy. Almost *too* easy. "How many more automatons are there?"

I could just barely hear the gears in its head whirring. So cool. "Only five more anatas."

"Anatas?" Maria asked.

"Automatons," Number One said.

Trent raised his ax. "Why only five?" he asked, then wheeled around and threw his ax into the middle of one of them. It fell into Maria's arms.

"No fair!" she yelled. "I had that one first!"

Trent smiled. "Where's your sword then, Correos?"

She flipped the automaton over. Her sword was lodged in its back.

"Cheater," Trent said, then they both ran toward the hole in the wall.

I turned back toward Number One. Trent was right. The number of anatas didn't make sense. "Why are there so few of you?"

"Scouting party."

"Wait," I said, "does that mean we've been scouted?"

"Affirmative."

"How many more are coming?"

"No orders yet."

"Will you know when the rest of the army gets their orders?"

"Directly after," Number One replied.

I watched Trent and Maria raise their weapons and crash into the last anata. When they finished it off, Asterion brought me over to revive it, and I explained the situation to them.

"Let's make for the portal," Trent said.

"They'll get clogged up there," Maria said.

"And we can obliterate them!" Trent yelled, a little too excitedly.

"Good idea." I waved the key in front of the fallen anata. Its leg twitched, and I tucked the key back in my shirt as Asterion settled me back on his horns. "We can finish them off before they even cross the threshold."

The anata jerked on the ground, then its eyes shot open. "Master?"

"Charlie," I replied, and pointed it toward Number One.

"Little warriors," Asterion said, looking over at Trent and Maria. "Who won the wager?"

"I did!" Maria said.

"No way!" Trent said, pointing at the last one. "I put his lights out!"

"Only after I put my sword in him!"

"Which I'm sure really messed up his—"

"Guys!" I said. "They'll be more. Lots more. Those were just scouts."

"*Pero,*" Maria brandished her sword in the air, "*I* killed the most scouts."

"Because you're a cheater." Trent kicked sand up at her.

She stuck her tongue out at him, and he kicked more sand in her face.

"Let's get going," I said. Over fifty sets of eyes flashed and turned toward me, pincers in the air. I realized I was addressing an entire army now – or at least a platoon. "Move out!" I yelled, hoping that sounded right.

CHAPTER ELEVEN

The anatas immediately formed a line, and Asterion pushed me to the front of it. I could still hear Trent and Maria fighting somewhere behind us.

Well, fighting wasn't quite the right word. They weren't really fighting anymore. I mean, they were yelling at each other, and they were shoving each other too, but they were being *nice* about it. I know – it sounds weird. But they were finally getting along again.

I relaxed back into my chair for the march through the labyrinth. Asterion started to walk down the path, but Number One stopped him with a golden pincer.

"Charlie," it asked, "would it not be more efficient if we went through the walls?"

I paused, staring at the brilliant sandstone walls. Part of me didn't want to do it. I was pretty sure that blasting through the walls of an intricately carved and beautifully crafted labyrinth seemed a little…well…wrong. And I could see Asterion tense up a bit at the thought too.

But Number One was also making a good point. It

would be quicker to blast our way through. And I don't remember seeing any giant labyrinth on National Geographic online. It was going to be destroyed someday anyway.

And we needed to get to my dad. I nodded at Number One and pointed toward the wall.

Number One reeled back and smashed and crashed his way through the wall. "Awesome!" Trent yelled. The rocks blasted apart and the sand melted underneath its golden pincers.

We crossed through the hole in the wall as Number One blasted its way through the next one. I covered my eyes, trying to keep the sand out, and asked Asterion, "Is it hard? You know, watching everything you've worked on – all your art – get destroyed?"

"My art is not what you think. These walls are not just my canvas – they are my prison. I spend hours carving them, cutting into them, and bringing life to them. But while I do, I dream of a life outside of them. A different life. A better life."

"What do you remember? From before?"

"It was so long ago, but it is still burned into my memory. My childhood was far from perfect. Poseidon had Aphrodite curse my mother to fall in love with my father, the Cretan Bull. When my mother gave birth to me, she was disgraced. I was a monster. Half-bull. Half-human. They said I should be destroyed. That I would only cause death, pain.

"But she did not believe that. She loved me more than life itself. She would rock me, sing to me. I remember her voice – it was like the sound of the sun dancing in the skies."

I smiled as he spoke. My mom loves to sing. She used to sing me to sleep every night.

Okay, she still does. It's my favorite thing. Every night before bed, she pulls me into her arms and rocks me back and forth, singing songs she makes up about my adventures.

At first, they were simple and funny, just like Mom: I would go to the store and buy bananas for my monkey. We would walk Cordelia to the ice cream store for chocolate and Dorito sandwiches. Over time, though, the stories changed. They became more and more complex. They lost their silliness. Mom stopped performing, and she started building.

I would travel through a land of darkness, bearing the only light the people had ever seen. I would ride a dragon through the wilderness, clinging to its scales as it burst through the smoke of a volcano. I would sing into the night, creating a thousand angels that would rise into the heavens and watch over me while I slept.

Those songs lifted me up and held me close when my legs began to fail. They made me feel warm and safe and strong, and even the memory of them made me feel warm inside on that cool desert morning.

"Poseidon, though, he was furious," Asterion continued. "And Prom – for reasons I do not yet understand – convinced Poseidon to have a labyrinth built and to trap me inside."

Asterion stopped midway through the next hole,

touching the stone that had been blasted apart. "Thanks to Prom, I have lived most of my life behind these walls. And yes, I have loved some of it." His hand dropped back to my chair and he pushed me through the break in the wall. "But I have hated even more of it. If I could, I would break down every wall, every stone. I would destroy it all, until nothing remained but dust and ash."

I could see his anger in the tenseness of his muscles, feel it in the heat of his skin. "I'm so sorry." He had been trapped inside for so long. I couldn't even imagine what he was feeling.

He pulled himself up a bit straighter and his voice softened. "It is not your fault, little one. If anything, your father and grandfather have been more than good friends to me. They have tried to help me defeat Prom, tried to help me reach the castle."

As we crossed through another broken wall, I scratched my head. "That's what I don't get. Dad was here? He was a Clockbreaker too?"

"Of course."

"Then he knew I would be one too. He knew I would be offered that choice."

"Yes, he knew."

I could feel the heat rising in my face. "Then why didn't he *train* me? Why didn't he teach me how to fight, how to protect myself?"

Asterion scratched the side of his muzzle slowly. "I cannot answer for him, Charlie. He made his own choices. And there is much that he could not discuss. But Trent has clearly been trained. That is not all-natural skill. And Maria is obviously very advanced, too. They will be able to help you."

"You mean 'protect me,' don't you?" I said, clenching my fists against my chair. "They should be able to protect me?"

He paused and ducked down as Number One destroyed another wall in a flurry of slicing legs. When it quieted down, he said, "That is their job. They are the elite. They protect you. You cannot be expected to do everything."

"But I can be expected to do something."

"And you will. You *have*. Not all battles are fought with swords. Do not underestimate yourself."

As the sand settled around us, I thought about what he had said. I *had* done a lot already. Reprogrammed anatas. Opened doors.

But, I still didn't think he was right. I thought I could have done so much more. If Dad had just taught me.

Think about it. Geography. Ancient History. Maybe even cartography. There is so much he could have shown me. How to throw knives. Shoot a bow and arrow. Something. If he had passed through so many doors, there was so much I could have learned from him.

Instead he spends all his time at "work" and I spent last summer redesigning my school's website and reading about HTML and PHP. Talk about useless.

Not to mention I had no idea how to use a weapon.

"I still could have used the training," I mumbled.

"Trent!" Asterion bellowed. He pushed me over to the wall, turned me around, and then let go of my chair.

Trent ran back to us. "Yes?" he asked, slinging his large

ax up over his shoulder.

"Teach her to use this dagger." Asterion passed the dagger down to me.

I caught the dagger in my hands and held it back up to him. "Come on, Asterion. This is stupid."

Trent looked at me, one eyebrow raised. I waved him away.

Asterion shook his giant head at me, his horns cutting through the air. "Make up your mind, girl. If you want training, he is the one you want. If you just want to whine, well, then perhaps I misjudged you."

I could feel a scowl crawling across my face, but I gritted my teeth and held it at bay. "Fine," I said, staring at the dagger in my hands. "What do I do?"

Trent knelt down beside me on the sand. "Okay. First off, you're holding it wrong. You want to hold it like you could immediately let it go. Like it could fly out of your hands."

He grabbed my hand and loosened my fingers around the dagger. I tried to ignore how warm his hands were, and how he was looking at me.

"There," he said. "How does that feel?"

"Like I'm holding a dagger."

"Good. Just don't put a death grip on it. You're gonna have to throw it."

"And how do I do that?"

"Easy enough." He held his hand out for the knife. I passed it to him, and he held it out to the side. "Always keep the blade horizontal as you throw. Your weak shoulder should face the target. Your body should be turned. You, well, you won't be taking a step—"

"Not without a miracle—"

He laughed awkwardly and stared down at the knife. "So, um, you'll want to make sure you put all your power in your throwing arm. Like this." He threw the knife, and it whizzed past Asterion, almost nicking him, then sticking in the wall, blade first.

I smiled. It was a good throw.

Asterion whipped around. "I am not the target!" he yelled at Trent.

"If you were, you giant cow, I would have hit you!" Trent yelled back.

Asterion snorted loudly. Trent bowed his head, but I could still see a smirk on his face.

"How do you know how to do that?" I asked.

"Practice." He wiped his hands on his pants.

"But how?" I asked. "With whom?"

Trent hesitated, and his words came out carefully. "My Mom's had me in dojo for the last few years. She thought it would be good for me to work out some of my…anger issues."

"Anger about what?"

"You know, my dad, the divorce…" He jumped up suddenly and turned toward the wall. "Mom was right. I'm less angry." He ran toward the wall and grabbed the dagger.

I didn't think that was necessarily true. Trent could barely hear his dad's name without spinning into a rage. I didn't get how learning to fight was going to make him *less* angry.

I didn't have time to ask him, though.

He handed the knife back to me. "Try it."

I took the dagger from his hand, grabbed my legs, and very deliberately pulled them away from Asterion. I definitely was not going to use a living target – not if I wanted them to keep living. I had absolutely no idea what I was doing.

I focused in on a torch bracket that was about five feet away – I figured I'd start easy. I pulled my arm back and worked on keeping the knife horizontal. It felt weird.

"Wait," Trent said, blocking my arm. "Try turning a bit more to the side. Don't directly face the target. You can get a little more power that way. Especially if you are sitting."

I turned a little bit, but kept my eye locked on my target. I drew my arm back and then quickly, with a flick of my wrist, I sent the dagger flying.

"Ow!" Asterion yelled.

My eyes searched for my dagger, but I couldn't see it anywhere. I swear, I threw it right at that bracket.

"I told you!" Asterion yelled. I spun around, and I saw it. Asterion was holding it up between his fingers, along with several pieces of his hair. "I am NOT the target!"

"Sorry," I said, but Trent just burst into laughter.

He stopped when I glared at him. Another wall exploded. "You…" Trent said between deep breaths, "could really use some practice."

I rolled my eyes at the obvious. Of course I could use some practice. But I clearly wasn't going to be practicing with *him*. "Maybe I need a better teacher."

Trent grabbed the dagger from Asterion and wiped it off, then handed it back to me. "You won't find a better one than me." He sat back down beside me again.

I stared down at his Reeboks, which were right next to my Chucks. "I've missed this."

"Me too." He cracked his knuckles slowly; I focused in on the sound of each pop. Then they were lost in the crashing and crushing of the walls. "Listen," he said. The crushing quieted down. "I'm sorry I've been ignoring you and Maria. I'm sorry I've been hanging out so much with Bobby—"

"I know."

"It's just easier. Bobby doesn't ask questions. He doesn't want to talk about feelings."

I thought about all those kickball games Trent had played this year. All those basketballs he had thrown.

"We don't have to, you know," I said. "Talk about it. Really. Let's not. Let's just be friends."

"Thanks."

I watched the dust explode upward as another wall fell apart. The wind hit our faces, brushing sand across our legs.

"Are we gonna be okay?" he asked.

"If we ever get out of this labyrinth."

"That's not what I meant."

"I know."

"Do you think it gets easier?"

"Being eleven?" I asked.

"Everything."

"I hope so."

"Happy birthday, by the way. Sorry your party sucked."

I wiped some of the dust off my jeans and looked back

at him. "I'm glad you were there. I'm glad you're here."

"Me too."

"Why did you come?"

"Because your dad asked me to keep an eye on you."

"Of course," I said, pulling myself up straighter. "Charlie Watch."

"He's just trying to protect you—"

"Come on. He's treating me like a baby. And now you're treating me like a baby. You only came with because you wanted to make sure I didn't hurt myself."

Trent's face got really red. "Fine. Yes. That's part of it. I can fight. And I knew I could help you. But that's not the only reason I came."

"Then why did you come, Trent?"

He pushed his hair back out of his face and, before I knew what hit me, I was staring right into his bright blue eyes. "I didn't want to lose you."

His words fell into me, making me feel wanted and warm and safe, like hot chocolate and a warm heating vent after a day of sledding on Richmond Hill. At the same time, his words made me feel dizzy and uncertain, like I was standing on the edge of something big.

Before I could respond, before I could find the right words, the key sizzled hot against my chest. I yelped and pulled it away from my skin.

"What's wrong?" Trent asked, his hand on my shoulder.

"The key!" I yelled, and just then Number One flashed up beside us.

"One hundred more Anatas," it said. "Plus, an additional five tranatas."

"Tranatas?" Asterion asked, suddenly by my side.

"Similar to the anatas," Number One said, "only faster. With better equipment."

Asterion's ears twitched. "What do you mean by better equipment? I've never seen—"

Suddenly the wall behind us exploded outward. Asterion was thrown back against the opposite wall. Quickly, he dragged himself back to his hooves and wiped the sand from his eyes. He reached down and grabbed the handles of my chair. I grasped my dagger tightly as I faced the wall to see what was coming. Three more anatas crawled out from the rubble, but they weren't like the ones we had been fighting. They had the heads and arms of humans, but at least ten sharp, spider legs with giant spheres where their pincers should be.

For a moment, I loosened the grip on my dagger, relieved that they didn't have those frightening pincers.

Then they charged toward us, and I forgot all about that.

They were fast. They slashed through our anatas – who tried to slow them down – tossing them aside like toys. With their razor-sharp legs and rapid movements, the tranatas split our forces in half. One tranata stood and fought the rest of our anatas, while the two others hacked their way toward me and Asterion. One of the tranatas slammed its leg down on one of our anatas, slicing it clean in half.

I knew Trent and Maria couldn't help me and Asterion fight the tranatas. They were already fighting off more anatas that were pouring through the wall, and there were at least two more tranatas we hadn't seen. It was just us. We were on our own.

I stared at the half-human spiders scuttling toward us, destroying our newly formed army. "I have to get near them!" I yelled to Asterion. "We can bring them to our side!"

He shook his head, and his giant horns sliced through the air. "We shut them down first."

"But they're destroying our anatas!"

"Then we will stop them. Place your dagger in your belt." He picked up several large stones and handed them down to me. They were like pebbles to him, but when he dropped them into my lap, I could barely lift them. I worked one up between both my hands and prepared to throw as Asterion clopped in front of me, and with a deafening roar, he charged.

Our anatas dove to the side as he barreled forward. Raising his mallet, he smacked a tranata into the air. At the same time, I hurtled my stone at the tranata's head, sending it sprawling. Running full speed, Asterion stampeded down the other one. The third one hissed and threw its front legs up. Thin webs sprung out of its feet, sliced through the air, and wrapped around Asterion's ankles. He flailed his arms, trying to keep his balance, but overcorrected and fell to the ground with a crash, spider webs tangled around his legs.

The tranata pounced. I ripped out my dagger as the tranata flipped through the air toward me. I sliced its chest, but it grabbed me with its humanlike arms. I tried to hold on to the arm of my wheelchair, but the tranata tore my fingers away, then climbed up the side of the wall, clutching me in its cold, metallic hands.

I batted at its metal chest with my dagger, hard and fast, but the dents made no difference. It didn't even seem to notice. It climbed on top of the wall and ran along the edge. I could see Asterion struggling to tear the webs off his hairy legs, and our anatas ran after us, but the tranata was too fast. It sped away from the battle with me in its arms.

It was too strong and fast for me to fight it. I could slow it down, though.

Tubes. They ran along the side of its neck. With how fast it was moving, I knew I only had one good shot. I grabbed onto its shoulder, like I was holding on for dear life – which I kind of was – then I lifted the dagger high and with a desperate yank, I ripped one of the tubes away from its neck and dug my dagger in deep.

The tranata's head whipped toward me and hissed, steam pouring out of its mouth as its red eyes flashed.

"Oops," I whispered. As it raised its other hand to grab my arm, I kept stabbing, sawing, cutting, until the tube suddenly burst apart.

"Erk?" it said, black goo flowing out of the tube and onto my arm. Its eyes flashed twice as it locked me in its steely grip. But then its eyes turned black, and its ten legs collapsed in a hiss of smoke and sand and dust.

It jerked to the side, and I held on tight to the dagger in its neck, my feet slipping over the side of the wall. Dangling. In the air. Fifty feet up.

"Asterion!" I yelled.

CHAPTER TWELVE

Our anatas streamed toward me, with Asterion in the lead with my chair. From up above, they looked like a delicate golden chain with a weird hairy pendant. My arms felt like Jell-O. Or pudding. Something mushy. Something that wasn't going to last very long.

"Guys!" I yelled.

I shouldn't have looked down. My vision spun and the ground flashed in front of my eyes. It was far. Too far. Asterion ran up to the wall, jumped toward me, and then crashed back to the ground. I couldn't get enough air. He was at least thirty feet from me. My fingers screamed, aching, gripping, sweaty. Too sweaty.

Suddenly, an anata flew into the air. It collided with the wall and came crashing down. I looked down and saw Asterion reeling back to throw another one. "Stop it!" I yelled, panting out the word, trying to find the air, but he tossed another one, and I cringed as it landed on top of the wall above my head. It scuttled above me, then reached out a golden arm and pulled me up, up, up into its arms.

"Charlie?" it asked.

My voice was stuck. My breath – somewhere in my throat. I wrapped my arms around its metal chest.

"Sorry we did not get to you faster. May I assist you?"

I breathed low and deep, pulling the air carefully into my lungs, then looked up at its face. It didn't exactly look like Number One. Its head wasn't dented in on one side. So it was strange to hear the same voice and the same kind words. The anatas were so polite when they weren't trying to kill you.

"Yes," I answered.

"I am going to transfer you to Asterion," it said. "He is waiting below. He will catch you."

The sureness in its voice calmed me, but then I remembered that Asterion was at least fifty feet below me. I opened my mouth to protest, but the anata's fingers let go, and I was falling through the air.

I gasped, but before I could yell, I landed in a pile of hair – Asterion's arms.

He held me up in front of his large brown eyes. "I thought I lost you," he said quietly.

"Not your fault," I replied, my heart still racing. "Where's Maria and Trent?"

Asterion pointed toward a rising cloud of dust and sand.

"You left them by themselves?" I asked as he shifted me back into my chair.

"Yes. They are the Elite. They protect you. They protect the key."

"They are my *friends,* Asterion. We can't leave them to fight all by themselves."

He nodded faintly. I couldn't see his face, so I don't know what he was thinking, but he pushed me back toward the battle without another word.

Number One ran up to us. "Maria and Trent!"

My stomach dropped. "Are they OK?"

"They are strong! They destroyed one of the tranatas." My head spun, and I swallowed quickly. I took a mental note to make sure and explain to Number One how to *not* freak me the heck on out.

"We have the other one trapped down that corridor," Number One continued. "No more anatas have been released. It is time to travel through the portal."

Number One took off, and we flew after it toward Maria and Trent, who were pushing a pile of busted anatas out of the way.

Maria squealed when she saw me. "Did you see us? *¡Luchadores!*"

Trent jumped in the air and high-fived her. "You were so fast! They didn't know what was coming!"

"And you were amazing!" Maria slapped him on the back. "You should have seen the way he fought, Charlie. Like he had an extra arm. *Increíble.*"

I smiled down at them both. "You guys were awesome!"

They were amazing. Faster than the speed of light. But—

But.

I didn't even want to think it. It was stupid, and it was selfish…but, well, I kind of wished I had been down there, fighting with them. Wielding a sword or hacking with an ax instead of doing a bunch of stupid reprogramming, waving a key, and getting kidnapped by the Green Berets of giant robot spiders. Oh, and getting rescued by an entire army while my friends fought by themselves.

So epically dumb.

I ran my hand through my hair, remembering what Asterion had said. I needed to give myself more credit for the things I could do. Stop pitying myself and be part of the team.

I remembered what Mr. Anderson told me in gym class after all those push-ups: You don't get to be the Incredible Hulk every time – sometimes you have to be Bruce Banner.

I smiled really big at Maria. Being Bruce Banner was not my favorite.

"You guys really were great," I said again, meaning it a little bit more. "But we're not done yet. We have to get through that door. Asterion and I will lead. Maria, you and Trent follow with the anatas in the rear. Stay close."

"Yes, sir!" Maria yelled, then started giggling.

I smiled. A real smile this time. I was being stupid. Everything was going great. We were almost to the castle. We were almost to my dad.

Asterion rolled me over the broken stone wall, hazy light filling the air. I squinted and saw the glowing blue portal. On the other side – through a shimmer like etched glass – a hallway emerged, lined by large grey stones. "The castle," I whispered.

I braced myself as Asterion moved us toward the blue light. I wondered what it would feel like to—

The wall exploded behind us, spraying sand and rock,

and a tranata blasted toward us.

Asterion dove to the side and grabbed Trent, tossing him out of the way and toward the portal.

Number One zipped over to us and crouched low by our feet.

"Go through!" I yelled to Trent. "Take those anatas! We'll follow!" He turned to leave, but then turned back again, his face determined. "Go!" I yelled. He nodded sharply and a group of anatas swept him through the portal. I turned back toward the battle. "Maria!" I yelled.

She appeared right in front of me. "You don't have to yell. I'm right here."

"Go," I said.

She spun toward the threshold, but a tranata leapt down from the wall and shot webs around her feet. Maria tried to break away, but it pulled her closer and started dragging her up the wall.

"No!" I screamed.

She was bouncing upward, just beyond our reach, screaming in pain.

"The portal is closing!" Number One yelled. Asterion pushed Number One through it and vaulted us toward the threshold.

I pulled at Asterion's hair, pounded on his hands. "Stop pushing! Get her! We can't leave her!"

Asterion paused with one wheel on the threshold, then fell into the light.

CHAPTER THIRTEEN

"No!" I yelled into the darkness. The light of the portal faded until it was just a dull outline on the wall that disappeared into nothingness.

The door closed. Maria. Gone.

"How could you?" I screamed at Asterion.

He stood still inside the tunnel, the sound of eight anatas whirring around us. He left her. Maria. He just left her on the other side.

I wanted to scream at him. To yell. To cry. Instead, I just clenched my fists and whispered, "Let me go."

He released the handles of my chair and silently stepped away from me.

"How could you?" I whispered.

"We had to get through the portal. We have no time. We need to get to your dad."

I could barely understand the words out of his mouth. He left her. He left Maria.

Trent pushed his way through the line of anatas. "What happened?" When he stopped in front of me, his face was pale. He spun around, eyes searching. "Where's Maria?"

I pointed up at Asterion accusingly. "He left her."

Trent sprang on him, beating him with his hands and fists. "She fought for you!" he yelled. Asterion just stood still, letting Trent beat against his legs, until Trent eventually got tired and dropped his hands to his sides. "You're a monster," he whispered.

Asterion shook his giant head, his horns scraping against the ceiling. "I had to make a choice—"

"And you chose wrong," I said.

Then it snuck up on me – déjà vu. Maria had said the same thing to me. She said I had made the wrong choice. When I took the key from Prom. She said I chose wrong.

And I suddenly knew how right she was. I made the wrong choice. I chose desire, need, and power. I didn't think. I chose the key. I chose myself. And now she was trapped with a tranata, heading who knows where, hundreds of miles away. All because I made a choice.

I looked up at Asterion, biting back the anger as I searched his giant cow eyes. He had made a choice too. A horrible choice. And we'd have to live with it. We couldn't go back and change it.

But we didn't have to let it change us.

"But this is where we are now." I gestured toward the dark tunnel. "And we need to get out of here, find my dad, and now we need to find Maria, too." I looked up at Asterion. "We should *never* have left her behind. I don't know how else to say it to you."

"We had to leave," Asterion said. "We were out of time. The door was closing."

I clenched my fists, tried to hold myself back. "That's what you don't get. It doesn't matter if the door was closing. We could have found another way. We don't just do whatever it takes. We're friends. We stand up for each other."

Asterion looked away, but I could see his horns bowing in the darkness.

I don't think he really heard me. There's no way it actually sunk in. But I was running out of time to change his mind.

Trent wiped his hands on his pants. "Let's go get your dad."

When Asterion bent down to push my chair, Trent blocked his path. "No way. You're not touching her. Not after that. Not ever. Number One, will you push Charlie's chair?"

Asterion hoofed the ground and kept his eyes on me. "You sure?"

I wanted to say something, something that would make it all better, but I couldn't form the words, even as his brown eyes bore into mine. I still couldn't believe he had left Maria behind.

He couldn't push me. Not when he did stuff like that. When he didn't even listen to me. When he took me where I didn't want to go. For one small moment, I hated him for wrecking my wheelchair. And for leaving Maria behind. But then I forced myself to let it go again.

This is where we were at.

I shook my head and broke my eyes away from his. I didn't want his help. I wanted Number One.

Number One skittered up behind me, and I heard his pincers lock on the handles of my chair. I pulled out my dagger and waved it in front of me. This time, I would be ready.

"This is better," I said.

Trent smiled over at me. "You look good with that dagger, Kleis. But don't think that means you're leaving my sight. We stick together."

"Yeah," I said, and he glanced away. Stupid Trent.

"Number One," I said. "We ready?"

"Affirmative," it responded. "It's two hundred paces to the galley, then six hundred to the throne room. I suggest three anatas go first, followed by you two and...the minotaur—"

"—Asterion," Asterion said.

"Asterion," Number One repeated. "Then the rest of the anatas. They will be expecting our return, but not yours. That will provide us with a tactical advantage. We have an eighty percent chance of reaching the galley unassailed—"

"That's reassuring," Trent muttered.

"—and a fifty percent chance of reaching the throne room without incident."

"'Without incident,'" Trent repeated. "It just sounds better and better."

"Guards?" Asterion asked.

"Thirty-five total. We should be able to disable them."

"Good," I replied. "But don't knock them out permanently. We're going to need them."

Three anatas led the way, and we followed. We scraped and padded our way down the tunnel, and with a start, I realized I hadn't even asked about Dad.

"Number One – have you seen my dad? Is he in the throne room? Or somewhere else in the castle?"

"I do not have that information. Anatas are not stationed inside the throne room."

I sighed. Of course they aren't. That would be too easy.

"How can we get Maria? When does the portal open again?"

"The anatas will bring her back to the castle."

"After we talk to Prom?"

"I predict we will do much more than talk."

"Odds?"

"Ninety-nine percent."

I wish I wasn't so good at math. It sounded worse as a fraction. 99/100. We were screwed.

The anatas opened a doorway and then paused before they crossed the threshold, pointing toward several spots on the floor. We avoided those spots as we made our way through – I wasn't sure why, and I didn't ask. I just trusted them.

I didn't hear any explosions or anything weird behind us, so I guess Asterion and Trent avoided them too.

When we reached the end of the dark hallway, one of the anatas stuck its head out the door. We watched and waited until it gestured with its hand. Then we slipped out of the tunnel and into another world.

It was like no other castle I had ever seen. Not that I had seen the inside of any other castles, but still, the floors, the ceilings, the stones – everything was made of gold. Golden candelabras reflected back golden light down an immense golden hallway filled with golden statues and golden vases with golden candlesticks flicking golden light on my golden chair. It was blinding.

"Midas," Trent whispered behind me.

I squinted into the light, and slowly nodded my head. The myth was true. King Midas. Everything he touched turned into gold. He must have touched Minos' castle, and everything else in it, including the anatas.

In our time, in our world, the castle would have been worth billions of dollars. Trillions. Even now, I don't have the right words to describe it. Except *golden.*

It was exactly what I think heaven must look like. Brilliant. Magnificent. Breath-taking. Really…shiny.

And I guess the sparkle distracted all of us for a moment, because the next thing I knew, we were being attacked.

Six anatas were scuttling down the hallway with large golden swords in their hands. Our anatas pushed out of the tunnel and quickly dispatched with the first two, but the other ones surrounded and decapitated two of our anatas and sliced the legs off a third. Asterion raised his giant mallet in the air and whacked two of them into each other. They collided in an explosion of metal and light.

Four anatas down. But we were making too much noise. More anatas would be on their way soon. "Number One," I said. "We need to get out of here."

Before Number One could respond, four more anatas scuttled down the hallway from the opposite direction.

"Tell our anatas to distract them!" I yelled to Number One over the crash of Trent's ax.

“Affirmative,” they all responded, without Number One saying anything.

I whistled to Trent and Asterion to follow, and we rushed down the hallway. Number One ducked in the first door we saw.

The room was dim, with boxes and barrels piled everywhere. We squeezed between two large baskets and Number One jostled one. I smelled the pungent scent of onions and garlic. Obviously, we had found our way into the pantry.

I could see a light at the far end of the room by the floor. As we got closer, I realized it was coming from underneath a door.

Trent slowly opened the door and ducked down. I ducked down too as Number One pushed me through. We made our way behind a long counter. At the end of the counter, there was a big table by a roaring fire with a giant, boiling cauldron inside.

Other than the tunnel, the cauldron was the first thing I had seen in the entire castle that wasn’t gold. It looked like a bubbling witch’s brew next to all of that shining stuff.

I suddenly had the inescapable urge to laugh. As Number One made his way into the hallway, I held my hand over my mouth.

Nothing about this made any sense. I had passed through a portal into a giant labyrinth where I met a half-man, half-bull, who liked books and didn’t eat me. We had fought and befriended half-human spider-robots, and made our way to a golden castle in a blinged-out wheelchair to fight some guy named Prom and save my Dad and my best friend. It was all so crazy.

Mr. Julian would have told me that the story didn't make any sense – that maybe I was leaving too much out, or I hadn't explained everything, and it was all getting jumbled at the end.

But he'd be wrong. That was how the story went. The path to find my dad – and even the reason why he was at that castle in the first place – was unclear to me. And as I sat in my new chair, at the door to the unguarded throne room, I realized that I really was missing an essential piece of the story. Something didn't make sense. But I couldn't put my finger on it.

Instead, I clasped the dagger tightly and glanced back at Asterion. He was standing behind me, his mallet raised. I turned back and Trent nodded to me, not even the trace of a smile on his face.

When I woke up the day before, I could not have imagined this was where we would be. But as I looked into Trent's eyes, I didn't feel scared at all. I nodded back to him, and he threw open the door.

CHAPTER FOURTEEN

The throne room was lined with black and gold chairs on our left and right, with black and red banners swaying high above them. On each chair sat a black ax and a red shield. A black carpet ran down the middle of the room, ending at a golden throne, which sat in front of a giant gold door. The door made my flesh ache, and the key turned red hot on my chest.

Where did that door lead? I wanted more than anything to open it, but the throne stood in the way, and on the throne sat a tall man, with a black wide-brimmed hat and a red cloak. In his left hand he held his golden staff. He looked up, and raised his right hand in welcome.

Prom.

"Asterion! My dear friend! It has simply been too long. Have you even seen my new palace? I've redecorated."

Asterion snorted. "Gold?"

"Yes," Prom said, surveying his throne room. "Midas owed me a very big favor."

Asterion leaned in to look at one of the black and gold

chairs, then knocked it over with his giant, hairy hand. "Tacky," he said.

Prom's eyes flashed and he tightened the grip on his staff. "I see you brought my Clockbreaker."

Asterion snorted again. "She is not yours, Prometheus."

I started at the name. Prometheus – Prom – the same guy from the stories. The ones Mrs. DePauw read to us. "Aren't you the guy the gods punished for bringing fire to humans? Didn't a bunch of crows eat your liver or something?"

Prom's face grew pale. "It was an eagle." He cleared his throat and continued, "And, I will admit, it was not my finest moment. But I've done so much more, even if I never made my way back into your stupid history books. And I've paid the gods back over the years, too. They've lost their powers while mine have grown. Their worshippers now kneel at my throne."

I didn't see anyone strewn about his feet, but his eyes sparked, and I figured now wasn't the time to say so.

His smile grew bigger. "And now that you're here, you can help me deal the final, devastating blow."

I didn't like his tone of voice. "I'm not helping you. That's not why we're here."

He laughed at me and then gestured toward Asterion. "Isn't it, Minotaur? Your precious girl? The one you've been pining for after all these years? Isn't that why you've come back to me?"

Well, that didn't make any sense. I looked over at Asterion for an answer, but he was staring Prom down.

"Ariadne," Asterion said. "Yes, she is the reason I am

here. I am here to pay you back because you did not even try to save her. You let her die. You saved Theseus and watched her drown." Asterion's nostrils flared, and he tapped the ground with one hoof.

"Still mad at me for saving your brother, eh? You guys never did get along. Well, I guess it's finally time you knew. She never drowned."

"But I saw her—"

"That fountain's a portal."

Asterion tilted his head, his horns swaying. "Is she—"

"Alive?" Prom asked. "Turns out she is, thanks to me. Fire of life and all that wonderful stuff. And that puts you in a different kind of position, doesn't it?"

Asterion dropped his mallet and exploded toward the throne. He grabbed Prom by the neck and thrust him into the air. "Where is she?"

"Ah, ah, ah," Prom wheezed. "Not so fast…Minotaur. You'll wreck…my new cloak. Besides…you can't kill me." He stretched out his neck and rasped, "I'm the only one who knows where she is."

Asterion slowly loosened his grip and dropped Prom back onto his throne. Prom adjusted his cloak and cleared his throat twice. "Thank you. I expect you won't be doing that again anytime soon." He straightened his collar, and Asterion nodded his head dumbly, his meaty hands balled into fists, but then he dropped his arms to his sides.

"Wait, what?" After everything he had said, after trying to convince me that Prom was the bad guy, and now he was on Prom's side? His head fell to his chest. Why was he giving up so easily? "Asterion!" I yelled at him. "What are you doing? What about my Dad? And Maria?"

He slumped beside the throne, his face unreadable, his brown eyes falling to his chest. He didn't respond.

"Don't listen to Prom," I told him. "You know he's a liar. You told me. His words are ashes. He's just trying to get you on his side. He doesn't have her."

It was like talking to a wall. He didn't even blink.

"You're looking at this all wrong," Prom said to me. "I never lie. I can help him. I *want* to help him. And I can help you, too."

"I don't want anything from you," I said. "I'm not falling for this again." I remembered how his tranata had dragged Maria away. How Dad had been chasing him. About the battles, the piles of broken anatas, and the stupid bottle of water.

"Yeah!" Trent added. "We don't need your help."

"Really?" Prom asked. "How do you plan on opening the Darkening Door?"

"You're just trying to trick me. I don't care about any stupid door. Where is my dad?"

Prom's head tilted to the side. "Looks like you do need my help then, do you not?"

"No," I said. "I need my dad."

"I know. And all you have to do is ask."

I kept my mouth closed.

"But really," he continued, "you didn't have to come all the way here. You could have just asked Asterion."

I didn't even look at Asterion. I just glared at Prom. "What do you mean?"

Prom smiled down on me. "Your father used his key

for the final time. He opened the Darkening Door. He made his final choice. Asterion knows that. Your father is gone."

Gone? Gone? The word screamed inside my head, drowning out my thoughts. "Gone where?" I looked toward Asterion and rubbed my eyes, trying to figure out what Prom was saying. "What does he mean? What's with that door?"

Asterion snuffed, kicking the rug beneath his hooves. I locked my eyes on his, refusing to back down. He finally responded, "I could not be sure. He said he was going to, but I did not truly know he would. How could I? And why would he go now? Why not wait for you?"

"Why indeed?" Prom asked, his eyes flashing orange.

"What's on the other side of this door?" Trent asked.

"Nothing," Prom responded. "Everything. It is the final door that the Clockbreaker can open. It appears in front of the Clockbreaker the moment a new Clockbreaker accepts the key. No one knows where it goes. Charlie, when you took your key from me, the Darkening Door appeared in front of your father. He opened it."

"Why?" I asked. The word tumbled out of my mouth. I couldn't believe it. I thought he was kidnapped. That someone had taken him. That's why we went through the whole stupid labyrinth. But in reality, no one had forced him to go. He *chose* to leave.

Asterion shook his head. "Your dad always said he would open the Darkening Door. To find out where it led and if it could help him stop Prom."

"I don't understand," I said slowly. "He knew what

Prom was doing? Why didn't he just come here? To the castle? Why not just fight him here?" My stomach churned like I hadn't eaten in days. I was beyond anger. I felt numb.

"I thought he was going to," Asterion said.

"Stop lying," Prom said. "You're not very good at it. You knew he wouldn't come back here. Not after last time."

I could hear Asterion gritting his teeth from across the room, holding back his words. He didn't say anything.

Dad was gone. And Maria—

"This has all been for nothing," I mumbled, running my hand through my hair. My fingers snagged, and I ripped them out. "He's not even here."

Prom clapped loudly, and we all looked back up at him. "It has most emphatically NOT been for nothing. You were the final piece – the last strand, let's say. I have completed my masterpiece."

My words failed me. Why was he so happy?

And why did his happiness frighten me so much?

"What masterpiece?" Trent finally asked.

Prom smiled, his lips stretching across his face, "Perhaps you should just see it," he said. Then he pulled a shining, pulsing, golden key from his robes.

CHAPTER FIFTEEN

"Another key?" Trent asked. "What is it with you guys and all these stupid keys?"

Prom's eyes flashed when Trent laughed at him and his key.

I wanted to laugh too, but Trent didn't see what I saw. He didn't *feel* it. Hanging from the golden chain dangling from Prom's hand was another key, yes, but it was not just any key. This one pulsed with dark possibility. It was like a gruesome car wreck that you can't take your eyes off of. Everything about it – the curves, the glow, the color – they all felt wrong. Terribly wrong.

But, at the same time, I wanted that key in my hands. Immediately. The desire was overwhelming.

"How?" I mumbled, watching the key absorb the light. "How did you make another one?"

"Can't you tell?" Prom asked. "I think the likeness is undeniable."

Asterion shifted uncomfortably and finally spoke from beside Prom's throne. "It is not—"

"Yes," Prom replied. "It is." My eyes were glued to his dark masterpiece. "Every part of it – its very essence – was taken from a willing Clockbreaker."

"That's gross," Trent said, wrinkling his nose in disgust. "You made that from people?"

Prom rolled his orange eyes. "You're just like your dad: so short-sighted. So focused on what's right in front of you. Missing the big picture." Trent's face turned red and he clenched his fists, but Prom ignored it. "You know how long it has taken me to make this key? How much work I put in? I have waited centuries for this moment."

"You waited centuries for that?" Trent asked.

I laughed suddenly, and the connection broke. I came up out of the fog. I blinked and looked at the key again. It was a key. Just a stupid key.

"You wasted your time." I shook my head.

Prom slammed his staff against the tile. "You have no idea what it's capable of. It will change everything. It is what I've been waiting for."

"Why?" I asked. "Why have you been waiting for that?"

"Because they would not give it to me!" he screamed, his composure gone. "The key! The key! It appears in my hands, but it never works for me! It only works once I give it to one of you—" His eyes reddened under his black hat, and he glared at Trent hard, and then turned back to me, his face twisted and contorted. "Disgusting Clockbreakers. It should have been mine! *I* should have been given the power to bend time and space. *Everyone* should have. It's just like the fire. The gods are always trying to keep everything to themselves. Daedalus was just playing right into their hands. And the Fates! They are always making sure that it's all done *their* way. With *their* rules. Which means I never actually get to use the key that I hold in my hand. I'm just a go-between. A temporary Clockbreaker. A deliveryman. The door behind me only opens to your world when the Clockbreaker reaches eleven years old. Your key appears in my hand. And then I have to pass it on. I am trapped here, or I am trapped there. I have no real power." His voice lowered, and he held the key up high. "No longer."

His words lingered in the air, and the silence afterwards felt thick in my ears.

Asterion broke it suddenly. "If you have the key, what do you want from her? Why don't you just open the door behind you?"

Prom's face turned pale. He stared at me hungrily. I gripped my chair handle tighter. "It needs one more thing. Nothing much. Just one drop of—" he raised his finger and pointed at me, "your blood."

"No way," I said, throat suddenly dry. "Not going to happen."

"But I need it!" he said. "To finish the key. *My* key. It needs that final drop of blood – the life and the magic within you – to activate it. To focus the power. I thought it would work with that strand of your hair, but it needs something more. One final spark. It needs you."

I didn't even pause. "I said no. I'm not helping you. You sent all those automatons to attack us. They kidnapped Maria. My dad has been trying to stop you. Why would I ever help you?"

It was like a light went on inside his head. His shoulders relaxed, and he smiled that awful smile. "You'll help me because of her. Maria. That is, if you ever want to see her again." My breath caught in my throat, but he wasn't finished. "And you'll help me because of your father. I'm the only one who knows how to open the Darkening Door."

I knew I shouldn't help him. He was just telling me what I wanted to hear. That's what he does – he tells everyone exactly what they need. He'd said all the right words when he gave me that bottle of Dasani. I'd listened to him, even as he'd faded in and out like a ghost or a hologram.

But there was so much more he hadn't told me. About him. About my dad.

I wouldn't help someone my dad had set out to destroy.

But I couldn't leave Maria either. And how would I open that door without him?

I tried to imagine another path, a different way, but I kept coming back to the same thing: He was right. I *had* to help him. I had no choice.

"Don't do it, Charlie," Trent said. "Maria wouldn't want you to. And neither would your dad. That guy is insane. You have no idea what that jerk would do if he was traveling through time messing stuff up."

What would Prom do with his power? All the good I planned on doing with the key – changing history, making things better – would he let me do it? Or would he make things worse? Would he start another war? Or would he end all the terrible wars of the past? What would he do?

I had no idea.

But once he released Maria, and showed me how to get to Dad, we wouldn't need Prom anymore. We could work together. Find a way to destroy his key before anything went really wrong.

For now, though, we had no choice. "I'll help you."

"You don't need to!" Trent said. "We can get them back some other way!"

Prom just shook his head slowly.

Asterion stirred, settling his large cow eyes on me. "Do you really want him to have that key? Do you not realize what he would do with it?"

"Silence!" Prom said, pointing his staff at Asterion. "Don't test me, cow. Or you'll never see Ariadne again."

Asterion closed his mouth slowly, his hands digging into his sides.

"It's my choice," I said. "And I choose to help him. But not for me. For Dad. For Maria. And for Ariadne." Asterion bowed his head, and I glanced back at Number One. He tapped his pincer, then we clicked slowly across the room to the foot of the steps. "How do I know you'll let Maria go if I do this? How do I know you'll help me find my dad?"

Prom grinned. "I always honor my agreements. Especially those that are paid in blood." He pulled out a shining golden dagger and walked slowly down the steps. I slipped off my dirty purple glove and held out my hand. He stopped before me, shooing Number One away.

"It's okay, Number One."

I heard him click back, and Prom took my hand in his own. His skin was freezing cold and hard. It made me think of a scaly fish. Or a crocodile.

I wanted to close my eyes, to think of some place far away, but I forced myself to keep them open. It would be over soon. Maria would be safe. And we would find my dad.

Prom raised the dagger, and I held my breath. He thrust it down, and I felt a sharp pain in my hand, and then I spun to the side. Trent rushed past me and threw his ax straight at Prom.

The ax sliced across Prom's face as he dove away, but not before a single drop of blood fell from my hand, landing on his golden key. Rays of light exploded out of it, and a shockwave of power hit me. I knocked backwards and almost out of my chair, but it sizzled hot, and righted itself. I couldn't figure out how – but then it didn't matter. Blood dripped down Prom's face as he held his golden chain in the air. The key dangled menacingly from it, glowing and shimmering and pulsing with power.

"Eliminate them!" Prom screamed.

"No!" I yelled. "You promised!"

His face cracked into a delirious smile as he lowered the chain around his neck. It glowed against his cloak.

Trent crawled to his knees and back up to his feet. He stared at my hand, dripping down blood, and his face turned a deep red. He grabbed his ax off the ground and ran at Prom, slicing the air.

Prom raised his golden staff up high; a flash of green light exploded toward Trent. Before Trent could land his blow, his ax melted and fell out of his hands.

That didn't faze Trent. He grabbed hold of Prom's staff,

then roundhouse kicked Prom in the stomach. Prom flew backward, but held onto the staff, and Trent went with him.

They landed back at the throne, and Trent jumped to his feet. Prom grabbed his leg and tried to pull him back down, and then all I saw was a whirl of motion: hands, feet, and legs flying.

Blood flowed down my arm, and I grabbed my glove and shoved it back on my hand. I clenched my own dagger in my fist and then pulled back.

I tried to find a clear shot – I didn't want to hit Trent. My dagger danced in my left hand, and when I saw a flash of Prom's cloak, I grabbed it and yanked him back as hard as I could. Prom fell beside my chair, and Number One sliced behind his knee with a golden pincer. Prom screamed in agony and fell to the side.

"Guards!" he yelled.

A side door banged open and a river of gold gushed toward us. At least twenty tranatas poured through the door.

"Now, Number One!" I screamed.

As he rushed us into the fight, I yelled over at Asterion, "Help us!" He just looked at me, desperation and frustration playing out on his face.

I had no time to convince him. Number One kicked one of his long legs out, tripping Prom for just a moment. Prom regained his feet and grabbed his staff. Green flames exploded out of its tip. He blasted Number One's legs, which melted instantly, collapsing.

My wheelchair spun and stopped, and I could see

Number One's feet melted to the floor.

I pulled myself back up and stared into the fire. Prom held his staff in the air, a green inferno swirling around his head. He pointed the staff at Trent. "You forget, little children, I wield the emerald flame – the source of life and death. I created man. And I create life. I am immortal. I cannot die. But you can."

He touched the golden key dangling around his neck. "The key is mine. You will never defeat me. And, if you keep resisting, I will go back in time and make sure you do not even exist." He slammed his staff against the ground and fire shot into the air. "Choose the easier path. Put down your weapons. We'll change the past together. Surrender your key, and we can create a new world."

I didn't want to create a new world – I just wanted my dad back. That was all I ever wanted. And look where it had gotten me. I was standing at the foot of a throne, negotiating with a madman who not only wanted to change the past, he also wanted to change the future. He wanted *everything*. He wasn't going to help me. He was only going to help himself.

Trent knew it too. In that moment, his blue eyes caught mine, and he looked at me with such sadness, such regret. I understood that look, and reached out to stop him, but he was too fast.

"Trent!" I screamed.

He lunged for the key.

Fire exploded from Prom's staff. Trent flew back into the throne. He knocked his head against it and crumpled beneath the throne. His eyes rolled back.

I tried to go to him, turning my wheels, and my chair jolted and jerked forward, but before I could even try to go further, Prom's staff was pointed at my face.

There was nothing I could do. I watched a line of blood tickle down Trent's face.

Asterion finally lifted his head, then pounded his fist into the ground, sending shockwaves across the throne room. He ran to Trent and knelt beside him, wiping the blood from his cheek. "Enough. She would never want this." When he looked up at Prom, his eyes were full of hate. "She would never let you hurt them."

He dug his hooves into the ground and charged toward Prom. His horns bore into Prom, and he lifted him into the air and sent him flying into the wall. Prom collapsed in a fit of coughing, but then, as he grasped his side, he hurtled a ball of flame at Asterion, sending him across the room and into a line of anatas. With a piercing cry, Prom swept his staff in a wide arc. The rug between them burst into flames, and a line of fire spread across the throne room. Asterion roared, the sound charging toward us, but he was trapped on the other side of the hall behind a blazing green inferno with an army of automatons bearing down on him.

It was just me and Prom.

"Now that the cow's gone," Prom said, grasping his stomach, "I'll take that key."

"But you said you'd help me," I whispered.

"The details of our agreement have changed." Prom straightened back up. "You have not kept up your side of the bargain. Your companions have been…very violent.

Besides, I can't have you following me. So give the key to me. Now. Or I'll take it from you."

I felt the weight of it around my neck, the way it pulsed, ached to go to the golden door behind Prom's throne. It called to the tranatas behind me – heavy and hot and powerful.

I had not wanted the key, and given the right situation, I might have given it up. It was too much of a burden; it carried too much wonderful and terrible possibility. I almost wished I had never held it in my hands.

But I wasn't giving it up now. And definitely not to him.

I reached down to protect the key, but just then, a rush of wind blew across my face, and the chain pulled out from under my shirt. I grabbed the chain tight in my fingers, but when I looked at the end of the chain, the key was gone.

"You mean this key?"

Maria was standing next to me, her hair disheveled and her jeans torn, but she had never looked better.

I would have hugged her if I could reach her.

"Give it to me," Prom said.

"No, *gracias,*" Maria replied. And with a rush of wind, she was gone.

Prom ran toward me, his silver staff raised in the air, spewing green fire. "I'll make you pay!" he screamed in my face.

I knew what I had to do. I grasped my dagger tightly and aimed right for his heart. I kept my weak shoulder pointing toward my target, kept my dagger horizontal, gathered my strength, and a surge of energy shot through my chair and out of me as I threw it directly at his arm with an earsplitting scream.

He shrieked like an eagle as it slammed into his right eye. He reached his hands up, tearing and ripping at his face with his fingers, but he couldn't get it out.

"This is not over!" he screamed. He whipped his staff around and ran from the room, green flames following him.

"Let's get him, Number One," I yelled.

"My legs are not operational," Number One replied.

"Maria!" I yelled.

"Yes?" Maria asked, right next to my ear.

I jerked away, then pointed toward Prom. "Get him! We can't let him escape."

The curtain by the door rustled, and Maria was gone.

I turned back toward the entrance. Asterion remained trapped behind a line of flames. And Trent—

Sprawled on the ground. Head bleeding. Eyes closed.

I couldn't tell if he was breathing. I pushed my wheels hard, and barely moved toward him. "Is he alive?" I whispered.

"My motion sensors indicate—"

"That he's a dork," Maria interrupted.

I swear – my heart literally skipped a beat. "Geez! Could you not do that?" I said. She glared hard at me. "Sorry. You surprised me again. Where's Prom?"

"Gone. No sight of him. It's like he disappeared."

I opened my mouth, but she shook her head. "I already checked the entire castle. Full sweep. I'm telling you, he's gone. I don't know where."

"I cannot detect him," Number One added. "He must

have taken one of the portals."

"Probably didn't want to race me." Maria reached in her pocket and pulled out my key. It shined in her hand. She held it out, and I grabbed it, slipping it back onto my necklace and around my neck again.

"Thanks," I said, feeling the warmth of it against my chest. It felt good to have it back where it belonged. "How did you get away from them?"

"I ran," she said, and then smiled and nudged my shoulder. Her smile faded as she stared over at Trent. "Wait—" she whispered. "He's bleeding." She ran over to him and lifted his head up off the floor, placing it in her lap. "You guys can't do anything without me, can you?" she whispered, staring down at his face. She poked him, and then smiled. "He's breathing. Just unconscious."

"Affirmative," Number One said. "He will awaken momentarily with an immeasurable headache."

Maria wiped the blood away from his face with the corner of her shirt.

I've never wished to be someone else more than in that moment. I would have done anything to be in her place. Instead I was stuck in a golden chair next to an anata whose feet were welded to the floor. All the while, she brushed the hair out of his eyes.

Then, a giant hand settled onto my shoulder. I took a deep breath, then let it go. "Thanks, Asterion."

He inclined his head.

I was so mad at him – I could feel it rolling over me. He had held so much back and left Maria behind – but I also couldn't imagine what he was feeling. Prom still had

Ariadne. Even though Asterion had finally made it to the castle, after all those years, Prom had slipped through his fingers. I reached up and touched his hand on my shoulder, gently squeezing. "You should have told us."

"I should have."

"We would have come anyway."

"I know."

"*Vámanos*," Maria said. "Let's go get your dad." She pushed her sword into her belt buckle and grunted as she hefted Trent onto her shoulder.

I shook my head. "He's not here. There's nothing here. I don't know why Grandfather sent us here. It was something about the automatons. We need to get back to him and find out what he knows about Dad. And the Darkening Door. And we need to get Trent to a doctor."

"And you too," Maria said.

I stared down at the blood that had soaked through my glove. It had dried, but it was going to *kill* when I pulled the glove off.

"Yeah, I should probably get my hand looked at."

We had so much to do – but my heart stopped as I felt the weight of Asterion's hand on my shoulder. I remembered what Asterion had said about the other portal, the one we had taken to get into the labyrinth. He said Prom had cursed him, trapping him inside the labyrinth.

I grasped his hand a little tighter. "What will you do? Will you come back with us?"

"I cannot yet," he said. "I have work to do here, first. I wish to do a thorough search of the castle – see if Prom left any clues behind."

"I hope you find her," I said.

"I hope so, too."

"We'll come back as soon as we can," I said. "But it may be a lot longer for you. You sure you want to stay?"

"Yes. I will find out where he took her. He must have left something behind."

"You will have more assistance," Number One said.

I stared down at Number One's welded pincers. "But how? You're stuck."

"The gold will melt and be forged once more. The reprogrammed anatas and tranatas are repairing themselves and returning to the castle. One is also available for your use. It can push you across the threshold. The additional anatas will release my pincers and repair them. Then we will search the premises for Prom. We will put out the fires. We will have further work to do with his remaining minions."

"I have an idea on that," I said. I heard a scraping sound behind me, and turned to see another golden anata crossing the floor.

"It is safe," Number One said. "It will help us. What is your plan?"

"Well, all the automatons are connected – they share orders, right?"

"Affirmative."

"Then we can strike back. A virus. A computer virus. I'm thinking that I could harness the power of the key to basically reprogram them all at once. If I can get back home, Grandfather can help me do it."

Number One's gears clicked loudly. It tilted its head to

the side, then nodded. "This will have to work. We must defeat them. They cannot be allowed to destroy this world."

"Let's go then, *chica*," Maria said, shaking Trent. "I'm sick of holding up this bag of rocks."

"Gentle, Maria," I said. "He might have a concussion or something."

"He better have one. Stupid, lazy boy."

I laughed but quickly covered my mouth with my hand.

Trent was so annoying. He was so mean lately. He had even followed me all the way to another world to keep driving me crazy.

But now he was unconscious and all I wanted to do was make him feel better. Stupid Trent.

"Let's go home," I said. The anata clicked up to me and locked its pincers on my chair. "Now, how do we do that?"

Asterion laughed. "The golden door. Behind the throne. It should open near your Grandfather's house."

I smiled up at Asterion. "We'll see you soon."

"You will," he said. "Be strong, Clockbreaker."

"Be strong, friend."

He snorted in reply.

I took that as a sign that maybe he was getting it: what friendship was. That we were a team. That we'd be back. And that we wouldn't let each other down.

You know, adults are slow like that. Even really big ones. It takes them forever to learn anything. And Asterion was, seriously, like the oldest adult I had ever met – by a couple of centuries at least.

I glanced back at Number One. "We'll be back."

"We will be ready."

"Let's go home," Maria said. "I'm starving."

"Yeah," I said. "I'm ready for some leftover cake."

Maria laughed. "You think they ate it without you?"

"You would have," I said.

She laughed even harder. "I already tried a piece. It's *delicioso*."

"What? Aunt Melda is going to be so mad."

"Nah. She'll just be happy you're back home."

We had been gone for so long. I couldn't even imagine what had happened at the party. Was Mom already putting on her benefit show? Was Grandpa okay? How were we going to fix all of this? Trent? My Dad?

The questions rolled over me as the anata scuttled us toward the giant golden door. I pulled the key out from under my shirt. It was warm, pulsing. It wanted to open the door. And so did I.

I reached toward the lock and slid the key in. My body thrummed, and then the key clicked. I pulled it back out, and the door opened, letting out a burst of light.

We were going home. Home to Grandfather. Home to Mom. And maybe, if we were lucky, we would find Dad too.

I braced myself against the shimmering light, and we crossed the threshold.

CHAPTER SIXTEEN

A bright light flashed in front of my eyes. I shut them tight, breathing in the wave of power flooding through me, flashing up my arms and into my chest. When I opened my eyes, it flooded out, slowly drifting away from me until I realized I was looking out at Grandfather's study.

"Charlie!" Grandfather yelled. He was sprawled on the floor, looking up at us, but as we crossed the threshold, his face turned ashen, and he spun away from us.

"Hold on!" he yelled, and tripped over his feet as he scrambled toward his desk.

"It's fine, Grandfather!" I yelled. "We're safe!"

"The automaton—"

"It's with me!"

Grandfather stopped scrambling, and turned toward me. I saw blood smeared on his chin and cheeks. "With you? How?"

"Are you okay?" I asked.

He pointed a shaking finger at the giant golden spider. "What is that doing here?"

"It's okay, Grandfather. We reprogrammed some of the anatas. This one—" I paused and tilted my head over its side, looking for its beady red eyes. "May I call you Number Two? Or is that insulting? Would you prefer something else? Like Julia?"

"The name Julia is agreeable. Thank you for naming me."

"You're welcome." I looked back at Grandfather. "Like I said, we reprogrammed Julia."

His eyes widened, then he smiled. "Of course you did. You're so smart. I wouldn't expect anything less. Did you stop the rest of them? The Cretans? And Prom?"

I tried to respond, but he talked right over me.

"And Maria! What's wrong with Trent? Put him down and go get Charlie's mother. Quickly, child!"

Maria set Trent down in a chair and, just like that, she was gone.

Grandfather laughed as he pulled himself up to standing. "Well, I didn't mean *that* quickly. I guess we will have to get used to her doing that now, too."

Julia rolled me over next to Trent, and Grandfather immediately stepped up next to the anata, examining the gears in its neck.

"Are you okay?" I asked. "Why were you on the floor? Have you seen Dad?"

"Unbelievable," he said. "That's a forged piston. How did he even—"

"Grandfather?!" I yelled, trying to get his attention. "What happened to you?"

"Quiet down, Charlie. I'm fine."

"What do you mean, you're fine? You were on the floor. You don't look OK—"

"Charlie, how long do you think you were gone?"

"Two days, at least. We only slept for one night though. We did a lot of walking in the hot sun. It could have been longer."

"Only *seconds* passed over here."

"Oh."

My voice caught and in the silence, I heard steam release from Julia, and then swirl into the air.

We'd only been gone for seconds on this side.

I thought Mom would be missing me. Making her posters. Preparing her benefit show. In reality, she probably didn't even realize I was gone.

Right on cue, she burst into the room, with Maria right behind her.

"Char!" she yelled, practically pulling me out of my chair as she drew me into a hug. "Did you take it? Is it yours?"

She could only mean one thing. "Yes," I whispered. "The key is mine."

"Oh, Char," she whispered into my hair. "I was so worried for you." She was rubbing my back in small circles, my head tucked under her chin. I relaxed into her and she rambled on, "Your dad and I wanted to tell you so badly. Since Manchester! But we couldn't! And then the Darkening Door appeared, and I tried to stop him, and I'm so sorry, but your dad took it and—"

Mom stopped suddenly, staring across the room at the anata. "What is that doing here?"

"It's okay, Mom. It's on our side. Its name is Julia."

"Julia. Okay. Got it. Right." She held me close, her arms stiff. "What happened to you? And your new gloves! And where did you get this chair? And what happened to your hand? It's bleeding!"

"It's just an—OW! Mom!"

She pulled the rest of the glove off and stared down at the cut. "It's not too deep. Won't need stitches. Maria, go get the first aid kit."

Maria disappeared and then reappeared moments later, hands full of assorted First Aid items. Mom took them from her hands, not even shocked that it took Maria only a few seconds.

Apparently, Mom knew exactly what was going on too.

"How'd you get this cut?" she asked, wiping the blood from my hand.

"Prom. He…stabbed me."

Mom's face went white. "I'll kill him," she said in a low voice. "Disgusting fire-eater. He would never…if your dad was here…" Her voice faded, and she pushed one big Band Aid into place.

"It's okay, Mom. We'll figure it out. Prom told us…the Darkening Door…we can help Dad…there's another way in."

She stared down at me, hands grasping my shoulders, her face alert and searching. "How? The door only appears when a Clockbreaker passes on the key. How can we get to him?"

I looked into her eyes, and my stomach wrenched. I had no idea. And I had let Prom escape. He was the only one who could help us find Dad, and I had let him get away.

"There *is* another way," I said slowly. "We'll find Dad. We just need to figure it out. Prom said we could. But he didn't tell us how."

Her face sunk, and she turned away. But before she did, I saw it. Frustration, and underneath, fear.

There was a sharp knock at the door.

"What is it?" Grandfather yelled as Julia tried to hide behind the couch.

"The cake!" Aunt Melda's voice came through the door. "And the ice cream's melting! Come on, Charlie!"

"We'll be out in a moment!" Grandfather replied. "Julia. Take Trent up the back stairs. Amelia, Trent needs to be looked at. He might have a concussion." Mom started and looked over at Trent slumped down in the chair.

"I didn't see him." She rushed to his side and felt his forehead. "Maria, go get your moms and meet us in the Rose Wing." Maria immediately disappeared, and Mom gestured to Julia. "Let's get him upstairs."

Julia lifted Trent and carried him up the stairs. Mom followed behind, then stopped at my chair and pulled me into a hug. "I am so glad you are safe, honey," she whispered into my hair. "And don't worry. We'll find your dad. I know it." She kissed my head and squeezed me hard, then disappeared up the back stairs. I stared at the doorway for several moments, listening for the way her feet hit the steps.

"She's a strong woman."

"She's going to fall apart. She has no idea what to do without Dad. We'll starve."

"We'll order pizza," Grandfather said.

"She tried to feed me uncooked parsnips last week."

"We'll get extra cheese."

I sighed, turning back toward Grandfather. He was adjusting his toupee in the mirror over the mantel. "What do we do now?" I asked.

Grandfather sighed too. "Well, we have quite a bit to talk about, Charlie. Now that you're a Clockbreaker, there is a lot more you need to know."

"Like how you hang out with minotaurs?"

Grandfather laughed, his toupee shaking back and forth. He stilled it with his hand. "Yes, like that. And lots more. Take your mother, for instance. You know why I sent for her?"

"Moral support? To have her perform her most challenging role yet: that of an attentive mother?"

"Don't underestimate her, Charlie. She loves you very much. But that's not what I was talking about. She has extensive first aid training."

"Mom?" I asked, seriously confused.

"Yes, your mom. She was always so worried when your dad came back through one of the doors all battered and bruised. She wanted to help."

"I never thought—"

"And that's the way she wanted it. She wanted you to have a normal childhood – well, as normal as possible. And so did your dad. That's why they didn't raise you here, no matter how much I argued with them."

My parent's choices suddenly started to make more sense. The way Mom always knew how to make me feel better. And the way Dad refused to accept Grandfather's gifts.

I had so many questions to ask Grandfather, like what did he think was behind the Darkening Door? And why didn't he open the door when he had the chance? And how had the automatons attacked him? And where was my dad? And was he going to be okay? And why did Grandfather send me through that door in the first place?

But it's like Aunt Melda has some stupid sixth sense. She always interrupts at the worst possible times.

She burst through the door. "It's time! The lights are out, the candles are lit, and we need this birthday girl!"

"The slideshow," Grandfather said.

I groaned.

"And your gift."

I perked up a bit. "Is it a pony?" I asked, smiling.

"It's better. Your dad—" his voice broke for a moment, but he pushed on. "We have been working on it. I don't think he would mind if I gave it to you now. I think he would want you to have it." He walked to the closet, a little unsteady on his feet. "Melda, we'll meet you in the living room."

"But everyone—"

"Can wait," Grandfather said, his back to her as he opened the closet door.

She stared at his back for a moment and then huffed and stomped out the door. "I don't know where you got that wheelchair, but wheel it into the parlor. In two minutes! Cake!"

Presents. Pictures. Cake. I really didn't want any of that.

I was wiped out. And it didn't even feel like my stupid birthday anymore. I thought I had spent my eleventh birthday trapped in an ancient labyrinth with a giant minotaur and homicidal automatons.

Turns out I had some birthday left. Three hours to be exact. But that didn't mean I felt like the birthday girl.

I missed my dad.

Still, I couldn't help but smile when Grandfather pulled out my present.

"Awesome," I said as he handed me a jet-black iPhone in a bright green cover.

"So you can always call home. No matter where you are."

"I will," I said. "As long as there's cell service."

He laughed, and pulled out a large black box. "There's more." He hung the box over the handles of my wheelchair. "This is a Bose sound system, with a built-in jack for your iPhone."

"Cool—"

"And it's also a solar charging hotspot…as well as some other things." He pulled out a small box and wrapped it around the right handle of my chair, then plugged it in behind me. "You'll get your own Wi-Fi wherever you go. And it has a charger for your laptop too. You're going to love it. There's a lot more it can do. But for now, if you see a button, please, don't press it. I'll show you tomorrow."

Tomorrow. If we could just get through to tomorrow, it would be okay. We had enough time because we could travel back through it. With the key, there was no stopping us. Grandpa would help. And Asterion too. We would find my dad, and maybe – just maybe – everything would be alright.

The slideshow, however, that was horrible. Pictures of me as a baby, pictures of me and Maria, pictures of me running over Trent's toes with my wheelchair.

You know, now that I think about it, I guess it wasn't all that bad.

But it was strange sitting in the dark watching this overview of my life considering how much everything had just changed.

It was all so different now. Maria could run faster than I could see, and my Mom was upstairs in the guest bedroom with a friendly anata. And Trent—

"Hey."

I started, and turned to the seat beside me. Trent.

"Hey," I said.

The wind blew past my face and suddenly Maria was sitting on the floor in front of me. "Hey," she said.

"Hey," I replied.

I looked back at Trent. "I'm glad you're okay."

"Me too," he replied. "Sorry we didn't rescue your dad."

The light of the projector reflected off his eyes in the darkness. "Me too," I whispered. His hair fell down into his eyes, and I reached up to push it back, but Maria nudged my leg.

"We're going back to the castle in the morning," she said, staring up at the pictures on the screen. "And Trent's mom says she's got some ideas for the virus."

Trent's mom. The programmer. My chest relaxed as my mind spun. We could reprogram the automatons. We'd have all of them on our side.

It wasn't just the three of us anymore. We had Grandfather. We had Mom. We had Trent's Mom. We had Asterion. And Julia. And Number One. With a little bit of work, we'd have an army of automatons.

We could get that stupid key back. And we could find Dad.

The music ended, and the slideshow stopped. My eyes settled on the final picture frozen across the screen. It was a close-up: all you could see was my smiling, laughing face staring into the camera. I was so happy.

What you couldn't see was my dad holding me up in the air, his arms outstretched, a pile of leaves around his feet. You couldn't see him smiling. You couldn't hear his voice. You probably wouldn't even know he was there.

I didn't want to be the girl in that picture. That image. Smiling, happy, but alone. Without a dad.

I wanted to be the girl who was flying through the air with strong hands beneath her arms. I wanted to be the girl who complained to her dad about her boring life and stupid friends over fried rice and noodles. The one who begged to not be treated like a baby while snuggling into her dad's chest.

Forget about the Black Plague, Global Warming, and all those massacres. If I could have gone back in time, if I could have used the key the way I wanted, I would have gone back for that. That autumn day. That moment. The feel of those leaves in my hair. His hands under my arms. His breath on my face.

I didn't want to change the world. I just wanted my dad back.

"We have to find him," I whispered.

Maria leaned back into my legs. "We will, Charlie."

"We will," Trent agreed. "And we'll bring him home."

The image on the screen faded to black.

In the darkness, I felt the key warm against my chest. Pulsing, calling to me.

I didn't care what door I had to open. What darkness lay in front of me. I'd open the Darkening Door. I'd go back in time. I'd change history. I'd give it all away. I'd do whatever it took.

I had to find my dad.

THE END

EPILOGUE

Number One flexed its golden pincers. They were brand new – thin and sharp. It could feel how the new pistons responded quickly to its commands. Number One felt like a new anata, just out of Daedalus' shop. If it had been human, it would have smiled at its newfound energy. Instead, it shifted the last of the debris onto the back of a tranata, who scurried out of the room.

The heavy lifting was done. The fires had been put out, and the throne room cleaned up. Asterion had been sent off on a quest for food. The plan was falling into place.

Another anata skittered up to Number One. "Charlie will return soon."

"Yes," Number One replied. "She will."

"What are our orders?" the anata asked.

"Yes," a voice whispered from the darkness. "What ARE your orders?"

Number One straightened up, new gears squeaking. "Same as before, Master."

A tall figure emerged from the darkness in a dark hat

with a wide brim and a shining red cloak. His right eye glowed with an emerald fire. The other anatas stopped their work and stood at attention.

"Bring the girl to Kells," Prom ordered.

Number One bowed slightly. "As you wish."

ACKNOWLEDGMENTS

This book would not be possible without the support of my friends, family, and writing community. The seeds of the idea were planted as my mom read Greek myths to me as a child. Watching my sister Tina's children grow and my friend Geneva raise her amazing girls gave me a new perspective and hope. My husband Bob supported me in so many ways as I figured out how to share the magic – he's always my biggest fan. I couldn't be luckier. And my son Rowan showed me what magic really is and made me want to create brighter worlds.

Each word I've written was crafted and cared for with the help of my writing community. The story took flight with my first writing group – thank you Amber James and Mimi Goldman! My friend Robert Monge read so many different versions of the story – thank you, Robert, for all the words you've read and all the stories we've created. I'm glad we found the best one. Mary Cummings gave me a chance, and my friends and colleagues at University of Oregon and Western Oregon University – especially

Maren Anderson, Matt Haas, and Miriam Gershow – encouraged me to keep sharing my work.

That's just the tip of the iceberg. The book you're reading – with Lee Moyer's captivating artwork – has been brought to you with the help of so many of my friends and fellow writers, including new friends in Portland and Willamette Writers. I am so incredibly blessed. Their names I'm holding in my heart, and writing in Clockbreakers Two!

But one more, before the last page. Grace Julian – my neighbor and friend – inspired me to write Charlie. Her strength and kindness continue to amaze me. She reminds me that it doesn't matter what age you are – you can do great things, and make the world a better place.

Keep shining, Grace.

ABOUT THE AUTHOR

Kate Ristau lives in a house in Oregon where she found a sword behind the water heater and fairies in the backyard. She is a folklorist who writes middle grade and young adult fiction, and continues to look for ways to change the world. You can join her online at Kateristau.com or follow her on Twitter @kateristau and Facebook @ristawesome.

CPSIA information can be obtained
at www.ICGtesting.com
Printed in the USA
FSHW021207261218
54693FS

9 780990 850755